To
the Periva Family

THE HERMIT'S MANSION

BOOK 2 of OCTOBERS

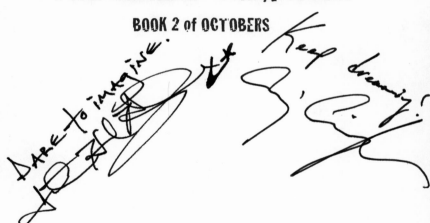

Dare to imagine.

Keep dreaming!

www.theoctobers.com

MOONSUNG

presents

THE HERMIT'S MANSION

BOOK 2 of OCTOBERS

FROM THE IMAGINATIONS OF

J.H. REYNOLDS AND CRAIG CUNNINGHAM

Illustrations by J.R. FLEMING

ISBN 978-0615544786

Dedicated to our teachers,
whom we have never forgotten.

CONTENTS

In the town of Hobble, October never ends . . .

THE HERMIT'S MANSION

BOOK 2 of OCTOBERS

31 Days Before . . .

Chapter 1:

A Match To Light The Night

Like every Hallows Eve night, the Stevens house sat dark and lifeless, bathed in silence while the rest of Hobble sprang from the neighborhoods and farms with wild merriment. Unlike most Hobblers, the Stevens' household did not celebrate All Hallows Eve.

Orson Stevens Jr., Director of the Ministry Of Light, waited outside in the shadows of his house for another group of trick-or-treaters to rap their knuckles on his front door. It was a monthly rite of passage in Hobble for every child to knock on Orson Stevens' door upon their first Hallows Eve without their parents.

"Trick or treat!" the young gang of costumed children cried out.

While the curious swarm inspected the front porch for candy, Orson Jr.'s deep voice thundered from the darkness, "Get off my porch! Members of the Light don't participate in such revelry! Nor should you!"

The children froze in their goblin-skin shoes and turned to see the dark-skinned man silhouetted by moonlight.

"We have never, and will never, celebrate this forsaken night!" Orson Jr. shouted. "Run along, you hooligans!"

The kids squealed and scampered towards the next house for better luck, dancing like merry ghosts beneath the orange glow of the burning street lanterns, and tossing handfuls of candy into the air so that it fell upon them like rain.

Upstairs in his attic laboratory, Starflyer Stevens heard the front door slam. He buttoned his labcoat and pulled his green-lensed goggles down over his eyes.

"Another group scared away by my father," Starflyer sighed as he continued working on the evening's project. "It's the same every October."

Starflyer's father believed such traditions were dangerous, even evil, and that the Living ought not imitate the Dead.

"Cheer up, Master Starflyer. Someday, you'll be grown up, and can go to the Star Festival if you wish."

Botty, Starflyer's robot, wheeled to her master's side. Starflyer had built her the year before from items gathered out of the town junkyard: an old apple crate, kyteboard wheels, spare sheet metal, pocket watches, and assorted coils.

"I wish I was grown up now," Starflyer dreamed aloud.

A gust of wind blew through the open skylight above. A stack of blueprints with diagrams for Starflyer's newest

2

invention swirled through the air then floated to the ground.

Starflyer climbed the ladder leading to the skylight. He sat upon the frame of the open window, and let the brisk October wind blow over his dark skin and fill the tail of his labcoat like a kytesail.

From the open skylight, Starflyer saw the lanterns of the Star Festival twinkling beyond Midnight Creek. As he smelled the sweet scents of Plumb's pumpkin pies and funnel cakes wafting through the air, the dazzling fireworks of the Hobble New Year celebration exploded across the star-filled sky and scattered into shapes of witches, vampires, and werewolves. Mayor Waddletub then lit a glitter cannon, which boomed a rainfall of confetti over the crowd and commenced the annual kyteboarding race.

Starflyer leaned his forehead against the window frame, and closed his eyes in longing.

"Master Starflyer, are you feeling ill?" Botty called up to the skylight. "You're acting quite strange tonight."

Starflyer opened his eyes and looked down at his friend. "It's nothing, Botty. It's just that—just sometimes— I wish I could be like everyone else. No one can possibly understand what it's like to be the Director's son. No fun. No games. No trick-or-treating."

Starflyer closed the skylight and slid down the ladder. He crossed the laboratory to a periscope, which hung down from the ceiling. The scope had two binocular eyeholes at its base and was connected to an old bicycle handlebar with adjustable knobs. The spying-device ran from the attic laboratory up through the Stevens' rooftop, and reached a dozen feet into the sky, where a glass lens magnified nearly everything in Hobble.

"I've officially missed 144 All Hallows Eves," Starflyer muttered as he fit his goggles into the viewing sockets of the periscope. "That's twelve years' worth—my entire lifetime."

Starflyer peered through the spy lens towards the Star Festival. The kyteboarders were wooshing around the second turn of the racecourse. Notch Cricklewood was in the lead, with Red Crisp a close second.

How could something so happy and full of light be evil? he wondered.

Starflyer then set his sights on the Crescent Gates, where Happy Gumbledump and Guffy Tinklepot rolled dice out of a bowler hat. The old men threw up their arms at the sight of double sixes and cheered for the fireworks exploding above the distant festival field, signifying the arrival of the Hobble New Year. Happy lifted a torch to light the twelve crescent lanterns, each lantern representing one month of the coming twelve Octobers.

Next, Starflyer turned the periscope and looked to the northwest corner of Hobble, where the Critchfield Mansion sat atop a hill like an enormous gravestone. The place had been empty for half a century, and was now the site of the most famous ghost story in all of Hobble. The man who had once lived there was said to have killed himself at the end of the Old War, and his ghost now haunted the manor.

As Starflyer looked towards the front door of the ghostly mansion, he saw a shadowed figure sitting in a rocking chair on the wraparound porch. The flickering light of a match revealed the man for a brief moment, and then all grew dark again, except for the faint embers of a glowing pipe.

Chapter 2:

The Portal Of Wonder

The next morning, Starflyer and Botty arose at dawn to fetch the *Hobble Gazette*, just delivered by Red Crisp. Evidence of the previous night's revelry was seen in every direction from the front lawn. Candle stubs still burned inside jack 'o lanterns, and the scent of caramel apples and cinnamon cookies hung in the air.

"I suppose your father will start another petition to outlaw Hallows Eve?" Botty asked as she vacuumed empty candy wrappers into a tube connected to her torso.

"You can count on it," Starflyer replied.

When Starflyer and Botty returned inside, his parents were sitting at the kitchen table. Orson Jr. was shining his shoes, and he immediately grew delighted at the sight of Botty.

"Ah! Now that *you're* here, you can finish glossing my

shoes while I read the *Gazette*!"

Orson Jr. tossed his loafers onto the ground in front of Botty and snatched the *Gazette* out of Starflyer's hands. He did not notice the horrific headlines printed on the front page.

"Dad, she's not a servant," Starflyer defended. The boy placed his hand on Botty's shoulder. "She's no different than you or me."

"Don't be ridiculous! We might as well put your little machinations to use. I have a whole list of chores for the bot, starting with raking the leaves."

Orson Jr. tapped Botty on the head with his pointer finger. "Did you hear that, Tin-Head? Rake . . . the . . . leaves!"

The antiquated clock on the wall chimed eight times as Starflyer's mother, Patty, removed a small wishbone key from her skirt pocket. She unlocked a wooden chest in the corner of the kitchen and presented Starflyer with his daily school lesson.

"Put that thing away," Patty demanded, nodding towards Botty. "It will only distract you. If you want a respectable apprenticeship at the Ministry or bank next year, you'd better start making better grades on your quizzes. Otherwise, you'll lose all privileges to your little workshop!"

"And we'll seal it shut forever!" Orson Jr. added on his way out the door to the Ministry Of Light. It was an old, and often repeated, threat.

Before Patty left for her job at the Hobble Bank, she turned and said one last thing to Starflyer.

"By the way, happy birthday! Your present is on the

table!"

She pointed to a wrapped box on the kitchen table, then quickly walked out the door.

As soon as the door slammed shut, Starflyer walked over to the small present and unexcitedly peeled off the wrapping paper, already knowing what gift he had received. He lifted out a box of unsharpened pencils, just as he had done on every birthday since he had learned how to write.

"It's a fine box of pencils, Master Starflyer," Botty said.

Starflyer tossed the pencils across the table and turned to walk up the stairs.

"Wait! You haven't opened your gift from me," Botty said with a smile.

The robot disappeared into the kitchen and brought back a chocolate cupcake with a single, sparkling candle on top.

"Happy twelfth birthday, Master Starflyer! I picked it up this morning at Plumb's Bakery," Botty said as she handed her present to Starflyer. "Plumb told me to be sure to send you her love. Though she was acting a bit strange, if I must say. Come to think of it, the whole town seemed strange. Maybe it had something to do with that giant crater in the middle of Town Square."

"Thanks, Botty. But you know we need to save every extra token for the SX12. No more expenses, understand?" he said, secretly pleased that Botty had been so thoughtful. He made a silent wish, and extinguished the candle with a single blow. "Now come on. It's time to start on our *real* work."

Starflyer and Botty walked to the spiral staircase leading up to the attic lab. The stairs were a portal into a world of wonder and freedom, far from his parents' world of duty and fear. With each step, Starflyer felt a rush of growing excitement within his heart, and a heaviness lifted from his skinny shoulders. He circled upwards until he arrived at the laboratory door.

"We're getting close, Botty. Everything will be different after we finish the SX12," Starflyer announced upon entering the lab. He lifted his labcoat off a nail pegged into the door.

Starflyer walked to a small slot cut into the laboratory wall, lifted a token from the cup below, and inserted the coin into the slot. As soon as the coin rolled through the opening, the attic erupted to life. A miniature train whistled as it rolled around a metal track, which wove throughout the laboratory, blowing out puffs of steam along its route. Wooden acrobat figurines slid back and forth across the room on livewires, tubes of chemicals descended from the ceiling on creaking pulleys, and intricate constellations rotated on the walls, pouring out of the candle tins and lanterns which hung throughout the room.

Starflyer sat down and devoured the chocolate cupcake. He glanced over at the bucket of tokens used to pay for his monthly lab expenses. It was growing emptier by the day, and he did not know how he would get enough funds to finish his recent project. At least, not for a few more Octobers.

"Now," Starflyer said, wiping the cupcake crumbs off his hands. "Where did we leave off, Botty?"

"I believe we had just decided that if we wish to excel past 537.392 miles per hour, the Light for the fuel tank must be *Unfiltered*."

Right then, unexpected footsteps echoed from downstairs and Starflyer held a finger over his mouth to hush Botty.

Botty rolled over to the coin slot and re-inserted the token, shutting down the laboratory with a dimming hum. She then retreated to a corner and covered herself with a white sheet.

Starflyer slid open his bookcase filled with chemistry books and went through a secret door to a shadowed hideaway. The young inventor plopped down on a chair and was instantly rocketed upwards by a coiled springboard built into the floor. His body launched into a dark, fitted cavern above, where a surveillance system of one hundred angled mirrors allowed him to view every room in the house. Starflyer squeezed his hand around the armchair lever and cranked it twice to reveal a view of the kitchen.

The kitchen door to the outside was wide open.

But no one was in that room.

No one was in his parent's room, his bedroom, or in the fireplace room either.

"False alarm," Starflyer whispered to himself. "Dad must have forgotten to close the door when he left."

Starflyer then clicked the armchair lever three times to the right until the mirrors reflected the attic lab itself. In the viewing mirror, Starflyer could see Botty hidden beneath the sheet, as still as a stone, blending herself into the various contraptions and schematics stacked against the wall.

Then Starflyer saw someone else in the lab.

Wearing burlap cloth over his head and hands.

Whispering something about a Time Crystal.

Chapter 3:

The Man In The Burlap Mask

The intruder examined the laboratory, lifting various inventions from cluttered workstations and inspecting them from every angle. The blueprint for the SX12 lay open on a desk, and the elderly intruder smoothed its crinkled pages as he studied the complex diagrams and equations. The man walked with a crooked cane and had a terrible limp. The strangest thing of all was that the man wore a burlap mask over his entire head—a cloth with two eye-holes cut out so he could see. There was not a hole cut out for his nose or mouth, but Starflyer could still hear him speak.

"Remarkable," he whispered in a low, gruff voice. Starflyer decided that the man's voice sounded like he was gargling rocks. "This invention would change the entire fate of Hobble."

The hooded intruder then noticed Botty's wheels

peeking out from beneath the white sheet. He placed the blueprint for the SX12 back where he found it, then crossed the lab. Starflyer then noticed that the man's large hands were wrapped in burlap cloth as well, as if to hide them. When the intruder lifted the sheet, Botty remained motionless and stared into his eyes like a lifeless doll. But he smiled back at her as if he knew her secret but was willing to play along with her game.

"Too bad," he said, winking his right eye beneath his mask. "She's just a toy." He re-draped her with the sheet and whispered softly, "There you are, now, darling. Nothing to worry about. I understand a thing or two about hiding."

Next, the intruder walked to the farthest wall and began counting the wooden boards of the attic floor, stopping abruptly at the twelfth floorboard. He climbed down onto his knees and placed his open palm on the splintered board with a sense of reverence, then took a small pocketknife out of his pocket.

He dug the knife in between the floorboards and wedged one of the boards upwards until it completely separated from the floor.

Out of the hidden hollow below the board he lifted a black, burlap sack.

The intruder untied the twine knot at the top of the bag, and peered inside.

"Safe and sound for all these years," he whispered. "Right beneath their noses."

He tucked the sack into his coat pocket, then stood to leave. But just before he exited the laboratory, the intruder noticed the slot in the wall and removed the token from the token cup, which hung below it. The man's eyes grew bright beneath the mask as he inserted the coin and the laboratory awakened to life.

"Talented boy! Just like his grandfather!" he exclaimed. "Destined for greatness, no doubt!"

The old man reached into his pocket and flicked a token into the half-empty bucket of funds for Starflyer's projects.

Just then, the kitchen door slammed downstairs.

"Son! Son, where are you?!" Orson Jr. called up the staircase.

The intruder quickly crutched toward the ladder leading up to the skylight. He ascended the squeaky steps before unlatching the window and escaping onto the rooftop.

When the room was clear, Starflyer sprung himself downwards from the Mirror Surveillance Chamber and burst out from behind the bookshelf hideaway. He could still hear the intruder's heavy boots thudding across the shingled rooftop. Botty frantically rolled around the room with the sheet dragging behind her.

"Master Starflyer! It was a thief! A thief has raided the laboratory!"

"I saw him Botty. But what was in that sack? He said something about a Time Crystal," Starflyer said.

Suddenly, Orson Jr.'s voice called from below, "Orson! Where are you, boy? It's urgent! Come down here immediately!"

"Stay here, Botty," Starflyer instructed. "I think we're in trouble."

Starflyer bounded down the spiral staircase three steps

at a time, certain his father had seen the untouched homework lessons. When he entered the kitchen, Orson Jr. was pacing in circles with his face buried in his hands.

"Dad, what's wrong?" Starflyer asked, concerned by the sight of his frantic father.

Orson Jr.'s bottom lip quivered as he looked up at his son. "Happy Gumbledump and Guffy Tinklepot have been murdered!"

"What?" Starflyer gasped.

"Murdered last night just before a meteorite crashed in Town Square! It's the talk of the town! Gather your things. I'm taking you to the Ministry for the day. I don't want you staying here alone! The murderer could still be in Hobble." He paused, then proclaimed, "The mark of the ⚡ has returned, just as I predicted. We must take refuge in the Light."

Chapter 4:

The Sealed Door

As soon as Starflyer and his father walked through the marble double-doors at the Ministry Of Light, they were overtaken by the outcries of frightened citizens.

I always hate the feeling I get in my stomach when I walk into this place, Starflyer thought.

The crowd edged toward the Book Of Members in the loft, anxious to sign their names into its keeping, thus protecting themselves from the dangers of the Vothlor. Until the murders of Happy and Guffy, most of the townsfolk perceived the Book Of Members and the Ministry Of Light as unnecessary superstition. But recent fears had driven many to look for protection in the most unlikely places.

Orson Jr. beamed at the sight of terror-stricken families and teary children pouring in through the doors of the

Ministry. He believed those who were most fearful were best suited for the Light, and served as the most useful kind of converts.

"At least something good will come of the town's troubles," Orson Jr. whispered to Starflyer as he straightened his bowtie. "And take off those silly science goggles. You look like some sort of bug. How many times do I have to tell you, Son? Appearances are *everything*," Orson Jr. then called out to the crowd, "Line up! There is space in the Book for all!"

Starflyer lifted his goggles onto his forehead, and watched his father address the crowd.

At the top of a narrow staircase behind the crowd was a golden book. The Book Of Members had been specially created by the Director who ran the Ministry before Orson Jr.—a man who had disappeared from Hobble during the Old War and never returned. After the Old War ended, the Ministry had shut down for many years, until Orson Jr. revived it. To many in town, he was a hero for bringing back the old traditions. A satin bookmark rested in the crease between two blank pages of the book, sparkling in the light of the hundred tiny candles which surrounded it. Converts could officially declare membership to the Light by signing their name with the crow-feather pen which sat next to a bottle of silver ink.

"Carrot-cake and cherry punch for those who sign! Courtesy of Plumb's Bakery! The best in Hobble!" Orson Jr. shouted as he squeezed his way up the staircase, offering consoling handshakes and blessings of encouragement to those who waited in line. "Become a Member Of The Light, and never fear again! There is enough space in the

Book Of Members for everyone!"

Starflyer stood still as the crowd flowed around him like a rising river. He took a deep breath, wishing he could be anywhere else. He turned and began to meander down the hallways of the Ministry—a place he had examined thoroughly all his life. He stopped to view the framed portraits of every previous Director of the Ministry, lined along a back hallway leading to the Director's office. He always thought it was strange that the portrait of the Director during the Old War—the Director who had created the Book Of Members and then went missing from town—had never been hung. Instead, an empty frame held his place on the gallery wall.

Suddenly, a chilling whisper crept around the boy.

"Maaaalivarrrr . . ."

Starflyer whipped around in the hallway, but he was all alone.

The wicked name dug into his heart, and goosebumps crawled up every inch of his skin. He knew the name well. His father always warned him of a dark vapor called Malivar, who would haunt his dreams if he wasn't a good boy. Starflyer looked for the source of the voice, but saw nothing out of the ordinary. He then realized that the whisper had come from behind the Sealed Door.

Impossible, Starflyer thought. *I must be hearing things.*

The Sealed Door was carved into the deepest recesses of the Ministry and had been left untouched for decades. As far as Starflyer knew, no living Hobbler had ever seen behind the massive stone portal. Starflyer had once asked his father what was behind it, but Orson Jr. swore he did not know. He said that the Director before him had given strict instruction to the town never to open this particular door, and that the Director during the Old War had been the one to seal it. Starflyer's father was not one to question authority.

The door had a symbol carved upon its middle—a circle surrounded by twelve dots placed like the numbers on a clock. Orson Jr. had called it the Sacred Circle, which he said was once used by warriors on their quests against the Vothlor.

I need to get some more sleep, Starflyer thought as he looked toward the silent door. The strange whisper now seemed like a hallucination of sorts. *Maybe Botty's right, and I'm working too hard these days.*

Just as Starflyer returned to the lobby of the Ministry, Kel Clovestar rushed into the room and tapped his polished cane on the gold-plated floor.

Kel called out in a trembling voice, "Mayor Waddletub has gone missing! No one has seen him since last night!"

Those in line grew silent. It was unlike Winky to be gone for more than a few hours at a time. All the Hobblers in the Ministry looked at one another like sheep without a shepherd.

"But I've a piece of good news too!" Kel continued, his voice turning joyous. "Lilla Humplestock is the interim mayor, and she just announced she'll give one-hundred tokens to whoever can move the meteorite! Says it was Winky's own idea before he disappeared!"

The crowd erupted with excitement at the opportunity for free tokens, and dozens of eager converts slipped out of line and hurried to Town Square. Starflyer listened in confusion as Hobblers spoke of Winky's disappearance and of a fallen meteorite. He sensed he had missed even more than usual this Hallows Eve.

"Dad, can I go try to lift the meteorite?" Starflyer asked, thinking it a good opportunity to make some tokens for his project.

"Over my dead body," Orson Jr. returned with a solemn stare. "That rock is evil, Son. Just like everything else from outside the walls of Hobble. From outside the walls of the *Ministry*, for that matter! Now move along, you're blocking the line."

Starflyer pushed his way through the crowd, imagining all the new equipment he could buy at Town Auction with a hundred tokens. He could even finish the SX12 this very October. Starflyer looked up at the platform, where his father smiled robotically at the handful of converts who remained in line.

I can't let this opportunity slip away, Starflyer realized, bringing his goggles back down over his eyes. *Dad will never know I'm gone.*

Without a second thought, Starflyer was out the doors and on his way to Town Square.

Chapter 5:

Evil Rock

A large crowd of mystified Hobblers had gathered in a circle near the auction stage, peering down at the meteorite. Their awestruck faces were bathed in the blue light pulsating from the crater below.

Starflyer pushed his way through the crowd and looked down at the fallen rock.

"I say it was put here by the Critchfield ghost! Any man who'd kill 'imself wouldn't hesitate to kill us as well!" Twilly Deathglow proposed.

"That was fifty years ago! Besides, there's no such thing as ghosts! If you ask me, this was probably Fink Karbunkle's doing," Nittle Nightbrook accused.

"Ain't true!" Fink Karbunkle defended. "We all saw it fall from the sky during the festival! Was probably sent by the Vothlor!"

"What do you say, Fizzler?" Babby Seedbottom called out to the back of the crowd.

The crowd parted, and a peculiar, wild-haired man stood with his hands in his pockets at the edge of the parted mob.

Zappy Fizzler was the specialist in scientific interests at the Hobble School Of Nonsensicals, and was also the town authority on astronomical patterns and variations. Starflyer had always admired Zappy, who had devoted his entire life to the mysteries of space and time. He watched as the absent-minded professor licked his index finger and held it up in the air, then closed one eye, and circled around the stone.

"It's from the sky, alright!" he concluded.

"We know that already, Fizzler. But what is it?" Babby questioned.

"I'm getting there." Zappy held his hands up to the sky, as if he were holding the entire universe in the palms of his hands. "You see, the constellations were rotating last night for the New Year, and one of the stars crashed through its own support system and fell towards Hobble, burning itself along the way at a temperature so hot it would melt us all like butter, and finally cooling when it landed . . . *right* . . . *here!*" Zappy stomped his foot as he spoke the final two words.

"Says who!" Twilly Deathglow challenged.

"Myself, and many other scientific authorities," Zappy proclaimed, then saw the lack of belief in the faces of the crowd. "Okay, just myself!"

The crowd closed in around Zappy and stood along the crater's edge. Starflyer watched as one by one, Hobblers tried to lift the glowing stone. It was half the size of a baby pumpkin, but no one could lift it—not even Nubb Plotterdub, the strongest man in Hobble.

"Who's next?" Mayor Humplestock cried out.

All of a sudden, Starflyer felt something ram into his back. He turned around to see Nash Ickleump staring back at him with his scarecrow grin and beady eyes. Nash wore a coonskin cap over his greasy shag of black hair.

"Watch where you're going!" Nash said with a wicked grimace.

Starflyer ignored him, as usual, and turned back toward the meteorite, only to find Mayor Humplestock pointing directly at him.

"You there! The boy with the green goggles!" she exclaimed joyously. "Come give it a try!"

Nash shoved Starflyer forward into the circle of townsfolk, who patted their new contestant on the back and urged him forward.

"Come along, boy!" Mayor Humplestock encouraged. "It won't hurt to try! There's nothing to be afraid of! You look like an intelligent young lad. The Director's son should have the wisdom to move it, if any of us can, eh? Let's see if you have the strength and wits to move this nuisance!"

Starflyer peered down at the cradled stone. Everyone watched as Nash sneered at Starflyer, "Ol' goggle-eyes couldn't lift a crow's feather! Much less the meteorite!"

Some of the crowd burst into snorts and giggles. Because Starflyer was homeschooled every day, only a few Hobblers even recognized him.

Mayor Humplestock offered Starflyer a welcoming

smile and motioned her hand towards the meteorite. "Go on! Give it a try!"

Suddenly, an intense wave of fear rushed over Starflyer. His father's voice haunted him: *That rock is evil, son.* He backed away from the meteorite and quickly pushed his way out of the crowd. He could hear playful boos and Nash's laughter as he ran back towards his house.

Though he had never been so embarrassed or disappointed in himself, Starflyer had figured out something about the meteorite.

He knew how to lift it.

Chapter 6:

The One To Blame

That night, wanting to take his mind off the day's humiliation, Starflyer went up to his attic lab to spy on Hobble. He peered through his periscope, observing the houses and shops across town, all alive with chimney smoke and candlelight, then focused the scope on one house in particular.

Starflyer noticed another flicker of light dancing against one of the upstairs windows of the Critchfield Mansion, silhouetting a black cat on the windowsill.

"So, you didn't even *try* to lift the meteorite?" Botty asked, breaking Starflyer's concentration.

It was the last thing he wanted to talk about.

"I already told you. No."

Botty remained silent for a moment, then replied, "We could have used the tokens. You could have at least *tried*." —

"Well, I didn't!" Starflyer snapped. "But I figured out

how to lift it."

A knock boomed on the laboratory door. Starflyer opened it and found his father waiting outside.

"Come down and see this, boy!" Orson Jr. ordered, impatiently. "Now!"

When Starflyer walked into the fire-warmed den, his mother was nestled in a hammock with her befuddled eyes locked on the Hobble Tube in the corner. She held a leafglobe in her hands, tossing it back and forth between her palms. Red, orange, yellow, and brown glitter-leaves fluttered within the tiny, glass ball. Orson Jr. joined Patty in the hammock, and motioned for Starflyer to take a seat next to the fireplace.

Mayor Humplestock's face filled the screen, and she spoke in a grim, but consoling tone, "Fellow Hobblers, as you already know, two of our dearest Elders have been murdered, and our beloved mayor has gone missing. In order to protect ourselves during these dangerous times, I am hereby establishing a New Rule: no Hobblers are allowed outside the town walls *for any reason* unless they have a signed gate-pass from me. This is for your safety. I have also raised the Danger Flag to HIGH ALERT, and the watchtowers and Crescent Gates will be guarded around the clock. Do not worry. Do not fear. All will be set right."

Orson Jr. turned off the Hobble Tube and paced around the living room. He added another log to the fire, filling the room with a warm flush of light.

"I've a guess or two at who's behind this awful farce," Orson Jr. said as the flames reflected off his glasses. "The Jypsi-folk! I say they killed our gatekeepers, left the mark of the **V** on the Gates, and kidnapped Mayor Waddletub. We can't trust them! Their unorthodox ways are a blasphemy to the Ministry."

"I heard someone in town today say it could be the ghost of Critchfield who's behind it all!" Patty chimed in. "Hermits and recluses aren't to be trusted—especially ones that kill themselves. Hobblers aren't meant to live their lives apart from the rest of the community like he did. Such people begin to think wild and forbidden things! Yes, Critchfield's the one to blame."

A thousand questions stormed through Starflyer's mind at his parents' rant of fear—but most especially at that name: *Critchfield.*

"There's no denying strange things have been happening all over Hobble," Orson Jr. continued. "Murders. Evil rocks. Just today, I thought I heard voices speaking behind the Sealed Door in the Ministry! I must be going loony!"

Starflyer quickly sat up on the couch.

"I heard something, too!" he said. "Maybe there's something back there. I've always wondered if—"

"You hush now, boy!" Orson Jr. commanded. "There's nothing and no one in there. The Director during the Old War assured the Ministry of it before he—before he disappeared. My ears were playing tricks on me, that's all. I only mean to say these are dangerous times."

"*Evil* times," Patty added, eyeing Starflyer.

After sneaking back up to the laboratory, Starflyer and

Botty climbed through the skylight and laid on the roof to watch the stars twinkling far, far away.

"It doesn't add up," Starflyer told Botty after pondering over the Monster Watch and his parents' theories about the Critchfield ghost and the Jypsis. "Something big is happening in Hobble though."

"Jypsis, Vothlor, and who knows what else. Maybe it *is* the restless soul of the Critchfield ghost causing all of the troubles," Botty speculated. "After all, you did see a strange light on his porch last night."

"Hey, Botty, look!"

Starflyer pointed to a hooded figure walking from Midnight Creek towards Town Square, creeping from one patch of darkness to the next until it arrived at the Museum Of Wonders. The cloaked figure ascended the museum's stone steps and snuck through the copper doors.

Starflyer and Botty exchanged concerned looks, then crawled through the skylight and slid down the ladder to the lab. Starflyer pulled down the periscope and angled it towards the museum. He placed his goggles into the sight-sockets and adjusted the handlebar knobs.

Through the museum's third-story windows, Starflyer could see a hooded man carrying a muffled light. Another shadowed figure walked beside him. Starflyer watched the duo pass from window to window, moving swiftly through the hallways. When they stopped at a room with an open window, Starflyer was able to see clearly inside.

One of the men was the old museum caretaker who had given Starflyer and Botty a tour several Octobers before.

"That's Pappy Cricklewood," Starflyer announced to Botty. "And—and—someone else, too. It's the man who

---

26

broke into our lab! Look at the burlap cloth on his face and hands! And his crooked cane!"

Pappy Cricklewood guided the masked stranger into a secret room and over to an ancient, leather-bound book inside a glass case. Starflyer remembered the book from his tour. He had been given special access to see it after inquiring about its whereabouts.

"The Time Journal!" he cried out, remembering that its strange equations supposedly told of the crystal once sought out by the Vothlor so that they could rewrite history unto the glory of Malivar. Starflyer remembered what the intruder had whispered in his room the day before.

In the shadowed room of the museum, the hooded figure patted Pappy Cricklewood on the shoulder as the two gazed upon the journal with a strange reverence. The hooded man lifted a black burlap sack out of his coat pocket and handed it to Pappy. Starflyer saw Pappy nod in understanding, then stuff the sack into his own robe pocket.

"He handed Pappy the same sack from the floorboards!" Starflyer added suspiciously. "Do you think it could really have the Time Crystal in it—I mean, the *real* Crystal?"

The masked man in the frock coat took his wrapped hand and hammered it against the glass case. He lifted the book from the display, tucked it beneath his arm, then shook Pappy's outstretched hand.

The museum turned as black as a witch's tongue, until a match briefly illuminated the darkness, and the glowing embers of a pipe pulsed in the stranger's hand.

Chapter 7:

The Junkyard

Several nights later, Starflyer waited until he heard his parents' bedroom door shut before he snuck out of the house.

He had reached the farthest edge of his backyard just as Botty drove up in a wooden cart with the word 'STARWAGON' painted on its side.

"I would be happy to drive," Botty offered, wearing her cherished railroad conductor's hat.

"Not tonight, Botty," Starflyer replied. "Now scoot over, please."

As Starflyer gripped the steering wheel and pressed the accelerator board with his foot, the Starwagon rolled forward, puffing out a trail of twinkling light.

"Master Starflyer, the purpose of this adventure is a riddle to me. I know we need as many free parts as we can find," Botty confessed, her mop-string hair blowing in the night wind. "But we both know a reactor box is all but impossible to find in the junkyard."

"We can't continue building the SX12 without it," Starflyer reminded as he turned a sharp left onto Darkwish Road. "Plus, we'll need the reactor box to energize the Powerclaw. If we lift the meteorite at night, no one will bother us."

The only opening in the town wall besides the Crescent Gates was the Junkyard Gate. Few Hobblers went near this place, not only because they feared the Lostwood, but because Darkwish Road ran next to the Critchfield Mansion.

"Buckle up, Botty!" Starflyer commanded as he lowered his goggles from his forehead.

Starflyer's eyes flared with excitement as he drove toward their destination. When the Starwagon reached maximum speed, he pressed a green button on the dashboard, causing six tight coils to spring out beneath the cart. Up, up, up went the Starwagon, just high enough to soar over the top of the Junkyard Gate. As soon as they cleared it, Starflyer pressed a red button, which released two inflatable cushions to soften the cart's fall.

"Works every time," Starflyer whispered in satisfaction, pressing a blue button to deflate the pillows. "Now let's find that reactor box, Botty."

"Like finding a needle in a haystack," Botty grumbled as she gazed up at the infinite piles of gadgets and toys and strange, shadowed objects.

In the deserted junkyard, towers of scrap wood and twisted metal reached into the midnight sky. Narrow roads weaved around the maze of junkpiles. Starflyer parked the Starwagon next to a heap of broken rocking chairs.

"Okay Botty, you check over there," Starflyer suggested as he shut down the engine. "And be careful. We don't want to be the next ones to go missing. Dad says Jypsis are always in the junkyard, stealing stuff."

Botty climbed out of the passenger's seat and rolled into the shadows.

At the nearest pile of junk Starflyer lifted up a small cone, and held it to his ear.

He heard a terrifying chuckle nearby.

The chuckler did not sound like Botty, or Dusty Bludpie, the junkyard operator. Starflyer crouched in the shadows as he moved in the direction of the voice. With the exception of a few ghosts, in all his monthly trips to the junkyard, Starflyer had never seen or heard anyone else there. A million fears flickered through Starflyer's imagination as he recalled Orson Jr.'s countless warnings about the Lostwood.

"Most Hobblers are ignorant to the truth of it," the croaky voice snapped. "And besides, they won't find out until it's too late! The Old Director has sent the instructions for Hallows Eve. Malivar will soon arise from his slumber, and the Vothlor will regain their powers. Once we have the other relics, Hobble won't stand a chance. And . . . you'll finally have our *own* soul."

Starflyer's heart thundered in his chest at the mention of the name 'Malivar'. He peered around the side of a burned stagecoach and saw two child-sized silhouettes digging through a nearby pile of junk, tossing some items into a wheelbarrow. One of the figures reached down and lifted a thick, metal chain from the pile. The other figure broke into a twisted laugh, which filled the night with a terrifying echo.

"Master Starflyer!" Botty cried out from behind the young inventor. She was holding a reactor box. "I found one! I found one! Oh, and it's perfect!"

"Shh!" Starflyer ordered.

He pulled Botty behind the toppled stagecoach, careful not to draw any more attention to themselves. A few silent moments passed, till Starflyer peered through the charred frame of the stagecoach once again.

The two figures were looking around for the source of the noise they had just heard.

Starflyer squinted to make out their faces, but could not see any distinct features in the dark.

"I heard it right over there!" the figure on the right growled, pointing towards the burned stagecoach.

Starflyer and Botty remained perfectly still. A moment later, they heard the sound of the chain being coiled into the wheelbarrow. He glanced through the stagecoach one last time. The figure on the right stood up straight and turned into the moonlight, revealing a haunting face . . . made of wood.

The wooden man jerked his head in Starflyer's direction, and fixed on him with black, painted eyes.

Chapter 8:

The Hand Of Darkness

All of a sudden, a rough hand wrapped around Starflyer's mouth and dragged him backwards.

I'm going to die! Starflyer feared. *I should have listened to my dad and stayed out of this place.*

His captor lifted him up and slammed him into the front seat of the Starwagon. When Starflyer dared to open his eyes, he saw Dusty Bludpie staring back at him with a fierce scowl.

"You ought not be here, Orson! This ain't no place for youngsters, you hear?" the junkyard operator ordered, checking over both his shoulders.

Starflyer looked up in relief at Dusty's grimy face.

The boy defended, "Yes sir, it's just I . . ."

"I don't need no 'scuses!" Dusty commanded, his eyes bugging out like two oversized marbles. "We's in a dark time," he whispered. "And creatures walk these parts that would love to eat up a boy like you, or worse, make you into somethin' you're not! Now get on outta here 'fore I report you to Sherriff for trespassin'.'"

Starflyer pleaded, "But we heard . . ."

"Get outta here!" Dusty commanded, pointing toward Hobble. "It's for your own good, boy, trust me!"

Starflyer pressed the wooden accelerator pedal to the floorboard and sped away, leaving Dusty in a trail of twinkling exhaust.

"At least we found what we came for," Botty said with a smile, holding tight to the reactor box. "Now we can finish the SX12 *and* lift the meteorite. What a night!"

"Hold on tight, Botty," Starflyer warned as he pressed the button which triggered the coil device.

The Starwagon soared back over the Junkyard Gate and bounced into Hobble.

"First we'll lift the meteorite, then we'll head home," Starflyer announced. "It won't take long now that we have the reactor box. I can almost taste those hundred tokens."

Botty pointed to a dark lump on the side of the road.

"Master Starflyer, look out for that boulder!"

Starflyer swerved the Starwagon to dodge the strange shape that lay at the edge of Critchfield's property.

"That's not a boulder," Starflyer replied. "It looks like—like someone's hurt."

The Starwagon slowed down as they drew near to the lifeless lump. The frayed bill of a cap and a pair of scuffed shoes revealed the unknown shape to be a boy. Starflyer parked the Starwagon and jumped out to help. The boy's body was facedown on the ground, and Starflyer tapped the unidentified stranger's shoulder to see if he was alive.

"Are you okay?" Starflyer asked, turning the boy over to see his face.

It was Nash Ickleump.

Nash opened his eyes and grabbed Starflyer's labcoat. He pulled him to the ground and jumped on top of him. The rest of the Numbskulls, Nash's gang of hoodlums, emerged from the woods and pulled Botty from the Starwagon.

"Well, looky who it is! I knew you'd stop to help. Always trying to be a hero, eh Orson?" Nash grinned, revealing his yellow, crooked teeth. He pinned Starflyer's shoulders to the ground and ordered, "I know you have it! Give it to me, or else she pays!"

"Have what?" Starflyer asked in fright.

"Don't play dumb with me! The meteorite—where is it?!"

Nash nodded towards Botty, and the Numbskulls brought her into view so Starflyer could see her being tortured. The Numbskulls twisted Botty's rake arm until it was about to snap.

"Meteorite?" Starflyer asked in fear and confusion. "I don't have it, Nash! I didn't even know it was gone!"

"Don't lie to me, Orson," Nash sneered. "It's missing from Town Square, and I know you used one of your stupid little inventions to lift it."

"I swear on Guffy Tinklepot's grave!" Starflyer cried out, worried for Botty's life. "I didn't take it!"

Starflyer tried to shake himself free, but Nash shoved him down in the dirt once again. "You lie! Here are your choices: You either give me the meteorite, or you owe me a hundred tokens. And if you don't give me either, your robot's gonna die."

"I'm telling you, I don't have it!" Starflyer yelled.

"Fine. Have it your way." Nash spit in Starflyer's face, then turned to the Numbskulls and commanded, "Destroy the bot."

The Numbskulls howled with laughter as they ripped Botty into a dozen pieces. They scattered her parts across the leafy ground, and the cream-white of her clock-eyes faded to black.

"No!" Starflyer pleaded. "Stop it! I don't have the meteorite!"

The Numbskulls kicked Botty's pieces across the ground and gathered around Nash and Starflyer. Nash lifted Starflyer off the ground and held him in the air.

"This is your last chance," Nash threatened. "Give me the meteorite, or we'll do the same to you!"

Suddenly, the wind grew more violent, and a ghostly chill filled the air. The dead leaves began to move and scatter across the dirt road, as if trying to run away from an oncoming predator. An eerie force moved in the nearby darkness as the Numbskulls circled around Starflyer.

Out of the darkness, a corpse-like hand reached out and clamped onto Nash's shoulder with a fierce grip. The Numbskulls turned, and became paralyzed with fear when they saw the nightmarish figure looming above them. The figure's head was covered in a burlap cloth, with two eye-holes cut out so that the man inside could see.

Starflyer did not wait around to see who, or *what* it was that had saved him.

He pushed his way through the circle of horrified

Numbskulls and dared not look back as the others shrieked in terror.

Starflyer slid into the Starwagon and ignited the engine. He slammed his foot against the pedalboard, and the Starwagon flung up dust and gravel as it fishtailed down Darkwish Road. The reactor box fell out of the Starwagon, but Starflyer did not stop to retrieve it.

When he checked the rearview mirror to make sure he was not being followed, he saw a tall, monstrous figure standing over Botty's scattered parts.

The Critchfield Mansion loomed behind the masked stranger.

Chapter 9:

Dust And Kindling

The next morning, Starflyer walked downstairs to find Orson Jr. reading the *Hobble Gazette* at the kitchen table.

"Where's your little robot contraption?" Orson Jr. asked without looking up from the article he was reading. "I thought you two were attached at the hip."

"She's—" Starflyer flinched, still shocked by the horrible sight of Botty's parts strewn across the ground. He had not slept all night, worried that his best friend might be gone forever. He planned to recover her parts as soon as his secret meeting at the Hobble School Of Nonsensicals was finished. "She—she needs some repairs."

"Hmph! I knew that hunk of junk would fall apart one of these days," Orson Jr. scoffed, as he tossed the *Gazette* on the table.

Starflyer looked down and read the headlines:

FOUR MORE KIDS GONE MISSING!
Nash Ickleump
Picky Flopp
Dimple Pimpleman
And Oakie Slugtroff

"Nash and the Numbskulls," Starflyer whispered. A second headline read:

METEORITE MOVED!
HERO HASN'T COME FORWARD
TO CLAIM TOKENS!

As soon as Orson Jr. and Patty left for work, Starflyer burst through the back door of the house and ran toward the Wagon Port, an underground cavern in the backyard where he kept the Starwagon. The caveport was covered by a blanket of leaves glued to a flatwood covering. Starflyer turned the crank on what appeared to be an ordinary water pump, but which lifted the covering.

A moment later, he was speeding toward the Hobble School Of Nonsensicals. There was only one man in Hobble who could answer Starflyer's questions about the missing meteorite, and its relation to all of the strange happenings in Hobble. It was a man who knew the complex patterns of the starworld as well as the back of his own hand.

Starflyer strode down the winding halls of the

—
38

schoolhouse to Zappy Fizzler's classroom. He peered through the stained-glass window and saw the schoolteacher mixing bubbling chemicals in a glass tube. The chemical reaction caused a small explosion, and thick smoke filled the room. When the smoke cleared, Zappy's white hair was covered with a layer of blue dust.

Starflyer knocked on the window, and Zappy turned in surprise. School did not begin for another hour, but Starflyer had gone early in the morning so he could have an exclusive meeting with the legendary astronomer. The wild-haired schoolteacher opened the door and welcomed Starflyer inside.

"Come in! Come in! I was hoping you would show up, young Stevens. The letter you sent me through the Breezemail sounded urgent," Zappy said, offering Starflyer a stool.

Zappy's classroom was filled with fantastical treasures. A petrified footprint of a mythical beast was displayed on one wall, two hand-written pages of the Time Journal sat in a glass frame, and endless diagrams of seasonal farming techniques, water purification devices, and weather control stations were pinned to the front of his massive bulletin board. Starflyer dreamed of one day becoming Zappy's apprentice, but Orson Jr. insisted science was for people with nothing better to do.

"I came to ask you about something," Starflyer explained, eyeing a small creature floating in a jar of gooey liquid on Zappy's desk. "It's something to do with the Beyond."

Zappy's eyes lit up like sparklers at the mention of the starworld. "Then you've come to the right place! Does it have anything to do with the SX12?"

"No, not today. I'm wondering about—about the meteorite," Starflyer revealed.

"Ah yes, yes of course! No one in Hobble can explain how it came or where it went." Then Zappy leaned in closer to Starflyer and whispered, "Except for me."

Zappy motioned for Starflyer to follow him, then led the eager young inventor to one of the walls of the classroom where a black constellation chart hung at a slant. The star patterns rotated, as if by magic, and Zappy pointed out how all the astronomical orbs were in disarray as a result of the fallen meteorite. Only one star remained constant in the midst of the stellar chaos.

Zappy pointed to the bright, white star and said, "This, young Stevens, is the Hobble Star. Fixed. Unchanging. Forever burning directly above the center of Hobble. During my youth, I often used it as a guide to find my way back from the Light Mines."

Starflyer interrupted, "My dad says the meteorite is evil. Is that true?"

Zappy began to stir chemicals into a pot. "As soon as someone claims the tokens, I'm going to ask Mayor Humplestock to donate the meteorite to the Museum Of Wonders. It must be preserved so Hobblers of future times may see it. Plus, I want to have it in a safe place for my own personal studies. It may have caused a terrible chain reaction. The balance of the starworld has been disrupted, and we are left to deal with the consequences."

"But if it *is* evil, then what does that mean?" Starflyer persisted, trying to connect the strange events which had taken place since Hallows Eve.

"If it is evil . . ." Zappy began, then climbed up a ladder to a bookshelf. He removed an ancient book with tattered pages and flipped it to its middle, reading a single line. He mumbled the words to himself several times before he slammed the book shut and concluded, "If it is evil, then it was surely sent by Malivar. And if that is the case, whoever took the meteorite doesn't know the great and horrible power they possess."

After Starflyer parked the Starwagon, he ran inside the house and rushed up the spiral staircase. He was anxious to retrieve his toolkit so he could collect Botty's parts from Darkwish Road and put her back together. But when he arrived at the attic door, it was sealed shut by crisscrossed boards.

"I told you a hundred times, your little laboratory is a privilege, not a right," Orson Jr. thundered from behind him.

Starflyer turned to see his parents, arm in arm, looking down at him with scolding eyes.

"Your quiz grades have been slipping. You haven't had a perfect score in a week," Patty added. "You need to refocus, Orson, or you'll turn out just like the rest of the hooligan children in Hobble. The Elders won't hand out the best apprenticeships to *that* lot."

Starflyer was speechless. His parents had threatened to seal off his attic lab a hundred times before, but had never actually done it.

"Plus, we found this." Orson Jr. held up the blueprint for the SX12. His father unrolled the papyrus document and re-examined its detailed diagrams with a scoff. "This is the kind of nonsense that can ruin a boy's life. Thank the Light this could never be built! It'd be the end of us all! Really, boy, your imagination is most worrisome."

"How did you—" Starflyer began softly.

Without another word, Orson Jr. tore the blueprint for the SX12 in half and proceeded to rip it up into a hundred tiny pieces. Before walking down the staircase, he turned to Starflyer and said, "Don't bother gathering kindling for the fire tonight. This will do the trick."

I live in a prison, Starflyer thought. *No one could possibly know what it's like to be the Director' son.*

Chapter 10:

Returning To Darkwish

After refueling the Starwagon, Starflyer backed out of his underground cavern and onto the midnight lawn.

He peered up at the Stevens' chimneytop, smoking out the final remains of the SX12 blueprint. He sped past his parents' bedroom window with a bitter grimace. The blueprint alone had taken twelve Octobers to complete, and the miniature prototype another twelve. He would need Botty's assistance and the missing reactor box before he could start the project all over again.

Botty.

With an anxious heart, Starflyer drove down Darkwish Road to the edge of the woods near the Critchfield Mansion. There, he stopped to search the ground, but not a bolt or a screw remained in sight. The reactor box was gone as well. The only evidence left behind was a faint trail of broken glass glittering in the moonlight, leading through the woods and up to the mansion. Starflyer followed that trail to the edge of the woods, where he was startled by the sight of a note pinned to a tree. The note read:

If you want her, come and get her.
I'll be watching, and waiting.
-C.C.

Starflyer's heart thundered in his chest as he unpinned the note with a trembling hand. A rusted, black key fell to the ground at his feet. He picked up the key and tucked it into his labcoat, then ran back to the Starwagon.

Starflyer drove up the dirt path toward the mansion. A massive, iron gate blocked the drive to the front door. It looked as if had not been opened in fifty years.

Starflyer inserted the black key into the keyhole of the gate. To his surprise, it opened.

The Critchfield Mansion stood atop the northwestern hill of Hobble, looking over the town with its cracked window-eyes, and sending wicked whispers on the wind to warn all Hobblers to stay far away. Starflyer drove towards the boarded-up house, feeling as if he were driving to his own grave.

After parking the Starwagon on the front lawn, Starflyer took a few steps up to the wraparound front porch, where wooden columns barely kept the house from collapsing. Just then, he noticed something shiny leaning against the front door.

It was Botty. All put together.

"Botty!" Starflyer whispered, moving closer. "Botty it's me! I've come to save you! Come on! We have to hurry!"

But Botty did not move.

As Starflyer stepped forward, one of the curtains in a downstairs window moved.

Someone was watching.

Waiting for him to come closer.

Without another thought, Starflyer lifted Botty off the porch and dragged her across the lawn, checking over his shoulder just in time to see the curtains jerk shut. He had just placed Botty onto the tailgate of the Starwagon and jumped into the driver's seat, when the front door of the mansion flung open.

Starflyer's heart pounded as he started the engine and raced back down the dirt road.

After parking the Starwagon, Starflyer fastened Botty to his back with a rope and climbed the drainage pipe up to the roof. He walked upon the shingles with silent footsteps, and unlatched the skylight.

Once they were safely inside the attic lab, Starflyer activated Botty with a robo-heart magnet designed to send electro pulses into her apple-crate Light chamber. She awoke with a sudden start and blinked her pocketwatch eyes in confusion.

"Oh, Botty, you're back!" Starflyer cried, thrilled to see his best friend alive again.

Botty peered up at Starflyer with a dazed look in her eyes and replied, "Master Starflyer, I just had the most remarkable dream."

Chapter 11:

Robot Dreams

"Lay down on the operating table," Starflyer instructed. "You can tell me the dream while I look you over."

"But I've never felt better," Botty responded, moving her various parts. "Though I wouldn't mind a thorough oiling."

Starflyer thought she looked shinier than normal, as if she were brand new.

Botty laid down on the worktable in the middle of the lab and stared up through the open skylight at the hazy stars above. The Hobble Star seemed to loom directly above the attic.

Starflyer took out a wirelight from beneath the table, which he looped through a metal hook hanging from the ceiling. The wirelight hook was programmed to move in response to Starflyer's voice, so he could use both hands without having to worry about maneuvering a light.

"Higher. Higher. Left. Stop," Starflyer commanded.

The wirelight hovered over Starflyer's shoulder and illuminated the robot below.

While Starflyer fastened two magnifying glasses over his goggles, Botty rambled, "It was the strangest thing, Master Starflyer. I dreamed I was held captive in a house. A magnificent house, much larger than any I have ever seen. It was haunted by a ghostly stillness and strange shadows." Botty paused, then continued, "There was another captive there as well. He looked like a, oh, I never saw his face—he wore a burlap cloth over it with two eye-holes cut out so he could see. But he lit a fire in the hearth and mended my broken parts in the firelight. He knew the proper placement of my every bolt and screw, as if he himself was the one who built me."

Starflyer wedged open the apple crate to look inside Botty's chest, where the compartment pulsed a green, eerie light. He found a tiny black box taped to the Light compartment, and tapped on it with his finger.

"You feel that?" he asked.

Botty winced, "Oh yes. I was warned not to remove the black box, if that's what you're touching. It's a Light reserve of some sort, I think."

"Interesting. Go on," Starflyer encouraged, intrigued by Botty's tale.

Botty continued, "The captive sat by my side, watching over me like the moon watches over the fields. Then, he held a mirror in front of me and I could see myself. All my parts had been mended! He had even combed my mop strings! He led me through the house, and made certain I did not stray off on my own. So many hallways! So many doors! All of them locked. I must have heard a hundred whispers echoing through those haunted halls. From behind closed doors came the voices of—" Botty paused, then whispered, "—of children."

Starflyer sat up straight and unhooked the magnifying glasses from his goggles.

"What do you mean, the voices of children?" he asked.

Botty continued, "Just as I said. Then he led me up a marble staircase. Up and up the stairs we went, towards a strange music, until he held me up to a window and I could see all of Hobble in the distance below. Only then did I realize that it was his home." Botty paused and looked up at Starflyer with her pocketwatch eyes. "The next thing I knew, I was back here."

Starflyer closed Botty's apple-crate chest, and unhooked the wirelight. The attic laboratory darkened.

Suddenly, Botty sat up on the operating table and turned to Starflyer with a startled look on her face.

"What is it?" Starflyer asked.

"I just remembered something else," Botty explained. "The reactor box is on the top floor of his mansion. My savior wants to give it to you himself. He said he wants to meet you."

Chapter 12:

An Escort Of Crows

Starflyer and Botty passed beneath the archway of leafless trees as they drove up the haunted hill to the Critchfield Mansion. Crows perched on the twisting arms of the trees and peered down with black, marble eyes at the boy and his robot. Jack o' lantern scarecrows danced in the fog of the nearby forest, swaying to the hum of the wind. If any of the Vothlor were hiding in Hobble, Starflyer thought this would be a good place.

Up ahead, Starflyer detected a dark silhouette standing between the curtains of an upstairs window.

Watching.

Waiting for him.

Suddenly, a flock of crows soared down from the trees and swirled around the Starwagon in a twisted dance.

Starflyer parked next to the rotting porch and gazed up at the forsaken, five-story house.

"Stay here, Botty," Starflyer whispered.

"I would rather come along with you than stay out here by myself," Botty admitted, jerking her head at every unknown sound. Her domino teeth chattered in fear. "I'll surely be eaten by ghost or goblin!"

"Sorry, Botty, but I need to do this alone," Starflyer resolved, taking a deep breath.

Botty trembled and ducked down in the Starwagon.

Starflyer walked up to the front door.

"H—Hello?" he called out in a faint voice.

A flash of darkness floated across the front windows.

"Hello?" Starflyer whispered, "My name is Orson Stevens the Third—"

The front door creaked open. An endless void gaped at him from behind the whining door.

"I—I came to—I came to thank you. For fixing my friend and for saving me the other night," Starflyer stuttered. "She also said you might—you might have my reactor box?"

The front door opened wider.

"Come in, boy," a deep voice echoed from within the house.

Starflyer flinched and looked back at Botty, who was crouched in the Starwagon and pretending to be invisible.

Starflyer stepped inside the entryway. A soft fire crackled in the hearth, providing the only warmth in the drafty mansion. Most of the furniture was worn and tipped on its side, and the floors were covered with thick dust. Across the entryway, two identical marble staircases curled up to the higher floors of the mansion. Starflyer could tell the house was at one time a place of beauty, and, perhaps, of happiness.

"Over here," the stranger's voice called.

Starflyer noticed a large figure sitting in a tall armchair in the corner of the room. But he could not see the man's face due to the shadows cast by two massive statues.

"I—I want to thank you. For helping my friend," Starflyer said nervously as he moved across the room.

The man stood up from the chair, gripping a crooked cane, his face still veiled in darkness. He took a few steps forward and turned into the dim glow of the moonlight pouring in through an enormous window.

He was the most hideous beast Starflyer had ever seen.

Chapter 13:

The Other Watchman

Starflyer cowered backwards, unable to look at the disfigured monster. The beast held the burlap cloths at his side, his face and hands uncovered.

"Do not fear me, boy. I am not what I seem," the hermit said in a half-choked whisper.

The firelight revealed the twisted features of the hermit's horrifying face. His eyes sagged at the corners, and his nose was flat and crooked, eaten away by scabs and sores. His milky eyes were hidden behind tufts of wiry-grey eyebrows, and he could only speak from one side of his mouth.

"I'm sorry—I didn't know—" Starflyer stuttered as he backed towards the front door.

"I won't harm you," the hermit promised. He held out his flaky palms to Starflyer as a gesture of peace. "Please, you can trust me. This is my home."

Starflyer pressed his back to the front door and felt for the doorknob. "I—I didn't expect—I didn't know," he confessed. "Everyone says you're dead."

The hermit attempted to smile with his crooked lips.

He cleared his throat and said, "Uncertainty is the cornerstone of belief. They don't know if I am dead, therefore they choose to believe it is true. It is a matter of convenience for them, and for me."

Starflyer considered the monster's words.

"My name is Crump Critchfield," the hermit introduced himself, then pushed back the long wisps of white hair which had fallen on his egg-shaped forehead.

Crump extended his hand toward Starflyer, who stood ten paces across the room. Starflyer crossed the floor with hesitant footsteps and gripped the old man's gnarled hand.

"I'm Orson Stevens the Third," he said, and shook Crump's hand.

"I know who you are," Crump mysteriously replied. "You're the spitting image of your grandfather when he was your age. Please, come with me. There's something I'd like to show you. I'll give you your reactor box when we get there."

Crump turned and hobbled into a nearby hallway, disappearing into the shadowy maze of his mansion. Starflyer remembered Botty's tale of the voices of children heard behind the locked doors. The crystal chandeliers began to slowly spin above him, and the house shifted with a deep growl.

Crump held a tin plate with a burning candle on it, and looked down at Starflyer with milky eyes.

"Now, come along. I only request you don't venture off by yourself. There are rooms in this place no one, not even myself, should enter."

Starflyer took a deep breath and followed as the hermit led the way into a cavernous hallway, turning over picture frames on hallway tables as Starflyer followed closely behind. They passed dozens of bolted doors as they weaved through darkened corridors and chandeliered chambers. Crump checked over his shoulder on several occasions to make sure Starflyer was not venturing off by himself.

Curiously, the most recent edition of the *Hobble Gazette* lay open on a hallway table, along with a dozen other clipped headlines. Starflyer stopped and spread out the newspaper clippings on the table. All the headlines Crump had saved were about the vanished children.

Each missing child's name was circled in red ink.

"Don't touch that!" the hermit demanded, staring at Starflyer from the end of the corridor. "Don't touch anything!"

Starflyer dropped the clippings and followed the hermit to a narrow staircase that twisted upwards to the towers of the mansion.

Could he be a part of the Vothlor? Starflyer wondered as he climbed. *Maybe he kidnapped Nash and the Numbskulls, and all the other kids . . . Am I next?*

A delicate music poured down the staircase from somewhere in the tower above. The piano played, paused, and played again, over and over as Starflyer climbed the rotting wooden steps toward the highest floor of the mansion. When Crump reached the top of the stairs, he looked down at Starflyer.

"There is no use running now," Crump called to him with a crooked smile. "Come in here, boy. I want you to see this."

The hermit passed beneath a canoe-frame doorway and motioned for Starflyer to follow him into the room. Crump lit six rows of candles from the candle he held in his hand. The enchanting music poured out of the room and filled the chilly air.

As Starflyer peered around the study, Crump stood at the opposite end of the room, looking out a moon-shaped window with his back turned to Starflyer. Two candelabras stood like guards at each of his sides, backlighting his deformed figure against the starry night.

"Please forgive the mess. I don't have many visitors," Crump apologized.

Rows of dusty books lined the bookshelf-walls, and a thousand others were stacked in knee-high piles all over the floor. On a nearby table sat an open music box, revealing a miniature-sized man and woman gazing at the star-covered ceiling of the box as the haunting tune played on.

"Come here, boy, I want you to see this."

Starflyer walked across the study and stood next to Crump. Through the window, the faraway orange and yellow street lanterns of Hobble twinkled like buttery stars.

"You aren't the only watchman in Hobble, young Stevens," Crump said proudly. "From here, I can see everything and everyone. And I can keep an eye on my Light Mines."

The hermit pointed to the tallest mountain in the range northeast of Hobble. The mining lanterns flickered deep in the Lostwood, spiraling around the mountain like a coil.

The Critchfield Family had made their fortune from the Light Mines, but everyone supposed C.C. Pottleman had taken over mining operations after Crump's supposed suicide. Everything about the Light Mines had always been a mystery to Hobblers. No one knew the details of mining operations and were left to their suspicions every time the Light Train delivered a new shipment to the Light Dock at the southern wall of town. Zappy Fizzler had often ventured to the mines in his youth and returned with outlandish stories about an underground world of infinite train tracks that wound like yarn throughout the entire mountain range. But hardly anyone believed him.

"Why haven't you ever come out of your house and told everyone you're still alive?" Starflyer asked. "Everyone thinks you killed yourself fifty years ago."

Crump lowered his cauliflower-shaped head and solemnly explained, "Let them believe what they wish. It suits me fine to be left alone."

"I—I saw you at the museum with Pappy Cricklewood. I know you took the Time Journal, and gave him the crystal," Starflyer said.

"Yes, it was a matter of utmost importance. He entrusted the old book to me, and I gave him a decoy crystal in case the Vothlor comes looking for it. They will believe they possess a great power, only to discover it is a fake. The real Time Crystal is in safe keeping."

An ancient grandfather clock rang out throughout the hollow mansion, reminding Starflyer of the late hour.

"I should probably go home," he said softly. "My parents will be looking for me."

"I suspect they will," Crump agreed. The hermit

shuffled across the room and lifted the reactor box off the mantel above the fireplace.

"These are a rare find," Crump said, eyeing the squared contraption. He tossed the reactor box back to Starflyer. "It's a miracle you found one. Or perhaps—," he paused and peered into the boy's eyes, "perhaps it was destiny."

The hermit walked back towards the Moontower window. He raised his withered fist, and pointed out the window.

"There is just one more thing before you go. Do you see the barn on the hill down there to the left?"

Starflyer looked down and saw a decrepit shelter made of driftwood. The roof had an enormous hole in its middle, and a family of crows nested in its exposed beams.

Starflyer nodded.

Crump continued, "It has been empty for many years, and I am too old to have any use for it now." The deformed hermit looked down at the boy and attempted to smile. "It could be your new laboratory, if you so wish."

Chapter 14:

In The Shadow Of The Puppet

Two days later, Starflyer parked the Starwagon outside the Light Factory in Town Square. The Light Factory sold and fitted blocks of processed Light to power the various electro-contraptions used in Hobble.

Meanwhile, a gathering was just ending at the Ministry next door. A steady crowd of Members walked into Town Square with dazed smiles stretched across their faces. Starflyer knew his father would soon be out to wave goodbye to his flock of Members, so he quickly slipped inside the Light Factory.

Immediately, Starflyer bumped into Asher Mottlebrew, the Director of the Mail Quarters. Asher nearly dropped the enormous device he held in his hands, but Starflyer helped him catch it before it fell. The iron octagon had four exhaust pipes and four flimsy tubes connected to its various sides.

"Sorry, Asher," Starflyer apologized.

"Not a problem," Asher assured. "You can jump ahead of me in line if you're in a hurry."

"No, it's alright," Starflyer answered. "What is this thing?"

Asher grinned. "Let me ask you something first," he started. "Do you ever wonder how mail arrives in the breezebox at your house?"

The mailman patted the contraption and nodded proudly.

He continued, "This Suction Generator powers the entire Breezemail system in Hobble. Requires a hundred blocks of Light a month. Greatest invention in Hobble history, if you ask me. As a matter of fact, it was your grand—"

Just then, Sistine Gockle walked out of the storage room at the back of the Light Factory and rang the service bell. The Gockle family had been the master alchemists of Light transformation in Hobble for a hundred years. Sistine, the green-eyed factory-keeper, was often thought of as the most beautiful woman in Hobble and had been crowned the Pumpkin Princess six years in a row. It was said her younger sister, Amber, would soon follow in her footsteps. Today, Sistine wore a dirty apron covered in rust chippings and grease smears from the various pieces of equipment she handled all day long. Her auburn hair was tied in a knot on top of her head and she whistled happy tunes everywhere she walked.

"Next in line!" Sistine called from behind the wooden counter.

Asher heaved the Suction Generator on the stone-top counter with a tremendous grunt, and patted it like he would a puppy.

"The usual!" Asher said.

"One hundred blocks it is, Mr. Mottlebrew," Sistine sang, then jotted down the order in her notebook.

Sistine disappeared into the back and then rolled out a chest of blindingly bright Light blocks which gleamed from beneath a long, white sheet. She toppled the blocks of Light onto the nearby weight scale, and a tiny, black arrow spun around the circular dial until it stopped on the number, "100".

"When will they be ready? I need the generator running by morning. The mail's piling up like a mountain."

"I'll make sure it's ready by midnight," Sistine replied with a friendly smile.

Asher tipped his cap and waved goodbye to Starflyer before he walked out of the Light Factory.

Starflyer stepped forward and looked up shyly at Sistine. He wiped his sweaty palms on his labcoat and took a deep breath to ease his nervousness.

"Next in line!" Sistine sang without looking up from her notebook.

"Hello, Sistine—I mean—Miss Gockle," Starflyer replied, nervously.

Sistine smiled. "Why, if it isn't Starflyer Stevens! I haven't seen you in two weeks! Where's Botty?"

"She's recovering from surgery. She's had a long week."

"Ah, I see. Give her my best. What can I do for you today?"

Starflyer cleared his throat and made his request, "I was

wondering if you have ten blocks of Unfiltered Light I could buy."

"Unfiltered again? I won't even ask what you're doing with it!" Sistine said with a smile and a wink. "We don't have any in the back right now, but the Light Train should be at the Loading Dock within the hour. Go on down there and talk to my brother. Tell him I sent you."

"Should I pay for it now? How many tokens will it cost?" Starflyer asked, politely, knowing good and well that Sistine never charged him for Unfiltered Light.

Sistine said, "You go on and tell Tog you've already paid for it. It can be our little secret."

Starflyer smiled and turned to leave, but froze in horror when he looked at the shop entrance.

Twister and Woody's painted faces shined back from the front door of the Light Factory. Twister held a wooden box in his white-gloved hands, while Woody stared at Starflyer with a vicious grimace and pointed his sharpened fingers at the boy's face.

"Get lost, kid," the wooden man threatened. "We have some private matters to discuss with Miss Gockle."

Twister lifted a chain from the box and draped it over his own shoulder with a taunting smile. Starflyer immediately recognized it from the junkyard.

Woody continued, "I would hate to see a nice boy like you get hurt. Now, scram!"

Starflyer hurried around Twister and Woody and slipped out of the Light Factory.

But instead of walking away as Woody had ordered, Starflyer cracked open the door to see what 'private matters' they had to discuss with Sistine.

He saw Twister carefully lift out a square, black candle from the wooden box and set it upon the order counter. Dark whispers filled the room—the same ones Starflyer had heard while near the Sealed Door at the Ministry—and he felt his heart surge with fear.

Suddenly, a terrible whisper splintered his thoughts, "*Maaalivaarrr.*"

He covered his ears, but the sound persisted. Starflyer realized that the voice was coming from the candle. Its black wick twisted upwards like a coil, and all four corners of the wax were as sharp as knives.

"Your brother has already told us he'll be with us when the time comes," Woody stated. "Will *you*?"

Sistine took a step back from the candle.

"I'll have no part in it," she declared. "You take this out of my sight and out of my shop right this instant."

"So be it," Woody whispered. "But you best not tell anyone, lest you wake in the night with your throat cut. Everyone must choose a side, Miss Gockle, and a time will soon come when you'll wish you had chosen differently."

Chapter 15:

Whispers Of Secrecy

Starflyer fled from the shop, intending to tell Crump and Botty all he had just seen and heard.

But maybe Crump knows more than he's telling, he thought, still quivering from the sound of that evil voice in his head. *Maybe he knows something about the Black Candle, and what's behind the Sealed Door in the Ministry."*

He climbed into the Starwagon and putted over towards the Light Dock. But the path through Town Square was blocked by a long line of kids snaking out of the bakery.

The wooden shop sign, which had always read *Plumb's Bakery*, had been replaced by a new sign which read *Gubbles' Goodies*.

Did Plumb sell her business? Starflyer wondered.

Starflyer drove past the line of kids. He recognized the

pink-gowned girl from the Candletin Inn standing nearby, and he slowed to ask, "You know why the line is so long today?"

The girl, Jezzy Jarman, replied, "Didn't ya hear? The Gubbles are giving out free samples of their new brew!"

"What does it taste like?" Starflyer inquired.

"Like nothing you've ever dreamed before. Like something—," she paused and thought for a moment, "— like something *beyond* dreams. At least that's what I've heard. I haven't actually tasted it yet."

Starflyer glanced back at the shop. Vivy Gubble waited at the entrance of the bakery, greeting children with a happy smile as they passed over the threshold. Starflyer breathed in the intoxicating smell wafting from the chimneytop and open windows of the bakery. The tickling scent was spicier than cinnamon, richer than chocolate.

Starflyer looked up at the Clock Tower to make sure he would not be late for the arrival of the Light Train. Glancing over at the Light Factory, he saw Twister and Woody crossing through Town Square towards Tobo's Toys.

Starflyer saw Twister rap on the front door. The Toymaster quickly stepped outside, looking over his shoulder at the wild gang of children inside his shop.

Tobo nodded towards the box. Woody opened it, and the Toymaster peered in as a wicked grin stretched across his sunken face. He took the box, shook hands with Woody, and went back into his shop.

What does Tobo have to do with those guys? Starflyer wondered.

Just then, a high-pitched whistle sounded in the

distance. Starflyer saw a shiny, steel locomotive pulling a dozen large mine carts roll atop the southern wall. Twinkling lights ran up and down the sides of the Light Train, and a glowing halo hovered above the rickety boxcars.

Starflyer was already driving to the dockyard when the Light Train came to a stop on the wall near the Crescent Gates. It held exactly what he needed to fuel the SX12, and to change the fate of Hobble forever.

Chapter 16:

The Candle Has Been Delivered

The clock attached to the front of the Light Train rang out eight times in unison with the Hobble Clock Tower, then the engine roared one final time before subsiding into a long, drawn out hiss.

The conductor of the Light Train slithered out of his compartment and somersaulted from the track platform down to the ground below. A short-brimmed cap sat atop his head and a black bandana was wrapped around his nose and mouth. The only visible parts of the masked conductor's face were his smoky, red eyes. He then lifted the bandana and blew the bullhorn hanging around his neck.

At the sounding of the horn, a crew of dockworkers unloaded the dirty blocks of Unfiltered Light from the box carts and slid them into wagons below.

Starflyer navigated his way through the dockyard, and ducked behind a wheelbarrow filled with chipped Light. He looked around for Tog Gockle's uniform of grey trousers and matching suspenders, and found him paying the train conductor for the new shipment.

The conductor spoke to Tog in a raspy voice, "I heard about the murders and the missin' tots. It's a piece of bad luck, it is. Strange things been happenin' at the mines, too, you see."

"At the mines? What's the news?" Tog asked as he counted the last tokens and placed them in the conductor's leather moneybag.

"Shadows in the sky, dark foxes in the tunnels. Some of the miners say there be witches at work."

"No such thing as witches anymore," Tog scoffed. "The witches are all gone. Hung 'em all at the gallows years ago."

"Ah, but maybe not all of 'em, you see. And even dead witches ain't truly dead. Especially the ones who have the mark. If Malivar returns, then who knows how many bodies he'll resurrect. With the missin' candle, no one knows what to think."

"What candle?" Tog asked.

But before the conductor could answer, one of the dockworkers blew a bullhorn from atop the train, alerting the two men that the Light shipments had been successfully transferred from the Light Train into the wagons below. The conductor took the bag of tokens from Tog and scaled the stones of the wall with the ease of a squirrel. A moment later, the Light Train growled back to life. The conductor hung out the window and tipped his cap one last time to the workers below, then disappeared into a twisting cloud of smoke.

By the time the air cleared, the Light Train was chugging back towards the distant mountain range.

Starflyer jumped out from behind the wheelbarrow and ran to Tog's side. "Excuse me, Mr. Gockle," he began. "I was sent here to ask you—"

Tog dismissed Starflyer with a wave of his hand, then walked towards the wagons being hitched to the horses.

But Starflyer stayed at his heels, "Your sister, Sistine—I mean, Miss Gockle—told me to find you."

Tog stopped and looked down at his silver pocketwatch.

"What is it, kid?" he asked with a sigh. "I've got a dozen wagons to get to the Light Factory within the hour. I'm working on a tight schedule here."

Starflyer nervously explained, "I'm just here for a bag of Unfiltered Light."

Tog removed his black, tri-corn hat and scratched his sweaty, golden locks of hair.

"Now, what's a kid like you going to do with Unfiltered Light 'cept get yourself hurt?"

Without even waiting for Starflyer to explain himself, the Dock Manager lifted a dirty block of Light from the wagon bed.

"Now, get on," Tog ordered, tossing the block of Unfiltered Light to Starflyer. "And don't come askin' again."

Starflyer thanked him and ducked beneath a wagon with the block of Light hidden safely beneath his arm. He was just about to reemerge on the other side of the wagon when he heard a familiar voice call out Tog's name.

Starflyer crawled on his belly beneath the wagon. He saw Woody and Twister's dusty coattails dragging on the ground as they approached the Dock Manager.

Woody leaned in and whispered, "The Old Director will soon be set free. His message is this: The candle has been delivered. Malivar will be here soon."

The Old Director of the Ministry? Starflyer wondered.

"I was wondering when you'd deliver the good news," Tog said, slyly.

Suddenly, the wagon Starflyer was hiding beneath lurched forward. He gripped the steel frame above him and hung upside down beneath the wagon as it rattled away from the loading docks and back towards the Light Factory.

As the wagon rolled into Town Square, the mysterious words rang through his head.

Chapter 17:

Light Into The Storm

Starflyer parked the Starwagon in the backyard and ran to the northwestern corner of his house. He lifted the lid to a metal box attached to the rain drainage pipe and pulled out a cup-like contraption.

Holding the device up to his mouth, he called up to the attic lab, "Botty, do you read me?"

Botty picked up the Wire in the lab and called back down, "Yes, Master Starflyer, I'm here!"

"Dive into the Painting Escape, and come down here now," Starflyer instructed.

"Are you sure I don't need more 'recuperation from surgery'?" Botty asked, still appalled Starflyer had made her stay home all day.

"Yes, and bring the Light Grinder with you. Oh, and make sure my father doesn't hear you. He thinks I'm studying for a quiz in my room."

A moment later, Botty slid out of a trap door and tumbled into a towering pile of leaves in the back yard.

"I'll never get used to that drop," she admitted as she tossed the funnel-shaped Light Grinder to Starflyer. "But I'd be happy to drive if you're feeling tired."

"Not this time," Starflyer denied, as usual. "You're still recuperating from surgery," he added with a little wink.

In Crump's barn, several of the wallboards were separated by six-inch gaps, allowing starlight to pour in between them and stripe the dirt ground. Rusted farming tools were scattered everywhere, unused for fifty years. Most of the windowpanes were broken and covered in dust. Starflyer shoved his way through a maze of spider webs and finally reached the center of his new workspace.

Botty stood in the doorway, afraid to venture any further.

"Are you sure this is the right place?" she asked as a mouse scampered past her wheels.

Starflyer placed his hands on his hips and gazed up through the open roof, which glittered with foggy stars. He turned to Botty and replied, "This is a perfect place to build the SX12. It's twice as big as the lab!"

Starflyer walked to the nearest window and looked out the broken glass toward the Critchfield Mansion. Crump stood silhouetted in the Moontower window, and Starflyer could even hear the enchanting tune repeating over and over again from the music box. His benefactor lifted his hand with a slight wave, and Starflyer returned the gesture.

"I need to ask Crump a few things," Starflyer said. "Like what he knows about the old Ministry before it closed down after the Old War. And about the Black Candle."

"There isn't enough time," Botty warned. "We better get started, Master Starflyer."

Starflyer bent down to pick up the Unfiltered Light and his Light Grinder. He lifted off its cover, revealing a broad funnel attached to a glass beaker. Inside the funnel were a thousand sharp metal teeth, which spun counterclockwise at the turn of the crank attached to its side. Starflyer pulled his goggles down from his forehead and cranked the handle as fast as he could. After carefully dropping a piece of Light into the tiny storm, Starflyer watched as it became pulverized into a shimmering powder, which sifted into the glass beaker below.

"The possibilities for this place are endless, Botty. If we can find a way to transport all of our materials from the attic lab, we'll have the first section of the SX12 built in no time," Starflyer said as he emptied more Unfiltered Light into the Light Grinder.

"Master Starflyer—" Botty tried to interject, but Starflyer was too absorbed in his vision to answer.

"We just need to clean the place up a bit, that's all," he continued. He lifted the beaker up into a stream of moonlight and inspected the twinkling substance. "To start, I can bring a broom from home so we can sweep the dirt away."

"Master Starflyer—" Botty tried again.

"And I saw some unbroken window panes in the junkyard last time we went. We can replace the broken ones and fill the empty spaces in the wall with the Muddy-Puddy we made last October."

"Master Starflyer!" Botty screamed.

Starflyer put a cork in the beaker and looked up at Botty.

"What is it, Botty?"

Botty cleared her throat and uttered, "I think now is a good time to tell you we have been followed."

Starflyer looked over Botty's shoulder, and his eyes widened in terror. There, in the shadow of the doorway, was the last person he ever expected to see.

Chapter 18:

The Last Man He Expected To See

Orson Jr. pushed Botty to the side and peered down at his son in baffled anger, and a touch of fear.

"You've really done it this time, Son!" Orson Jr. scolded, holding up his lantern to examine the barn. "What are you doing at this wretched place?! You could be killed! What if there were Vothlor hiding here?"

Starflyer hid the beaker of Unfiltered Light behind his back.

"Dad, I—I—" Starflyer stuttered. A million excuses passed through his mind as he searched for some explanation to calm his father.

Orson Jr. held up his hand to silence Starflyer, then fumed, "I looked through a window at the house just in time to see you driving off in that little electro wagon of yours. I followed your tracks, and found you here! At the

Critchfield Mansion, of all places! You should be ashamed of yourself! We have to get out of here before something terrible happens! Don't you know a man killed himself here?! Haven't I taught you to be afraid of ghosts!"

"But Dad it's not—" Starflyer began.

"Don't give me any more excuses!" Orson Jr. commanded. "You're coming home this very instant. What's that behind your back? Drop whatever it is you have there."

Starflyer revealed the beaker of Unfiltered Light, and carefully laid it on the ground next to his feet.

"Oh, for Hobble's sake, what is that?" Orson Jr. inquired. He walked across the barn and lifted the beaker from the ground, eyeing it from every angle. "I asked you a straightforward question, Son. What is this latest foolishness?"

"It's purified Light," Starflyer lied.

"Looks too dirty to be pure Light," Orson Jr. corrected. "Tell me what it is this very instant!"

Starflyer hesitated, then confessed in a quiet voice, "It's—it's Unfiltered Light."

Orson Jr. shrieked and dropped the beaker as if it were burning hot. The glass shattered upon the floor, and the spilled powder twinkled in the moonlight.

"Don't you understand that Unfiltered Light comes directly from the Darkness outside Hobble?" Orson Jr. huffed. "I've preached it many times before at the Light Gatherings, and will preach it till my last breath: there's no mixing Light with Darkness. It's either one or the other." He looked down at Starflyer and said, "I've never been more disappointed in you, Son. You're coming home with me, and you will never, ever, come back here again. Do you understand?"

"Yes sir," Starflyer whispered in defeat.

When Orson Jr. gripped Starflyer's arm and pulled him towards the door, he and Botty exchanged a defeated look.

"Come along, Botty," Starflyer said. "We have to go home now."

"Oh no!" Orson Jr. ordered. "You tell that *thing* to stay here and rust away for a thousand years. I won't have that contraption under my roof. She's corrupted you into hooliganism! And don't argue that its feelings will be hurt. It doesn't have *real* feelings. It's been nothing but a nuisance to your mother and me, and a distraction to your future."

As Botty lowered her head and retreated into the corner of the barn, Starflyer mouthed an apology to his friend.

While Orson Jr. dragged Starflyer towards Darkwish Road, the boy glanced up at the Moontower window. But Crump was no longer there.

Chapter 19:

A Nightmare Without End

When Orson Jr. told his wife about their son being on the grounds of the Critchfield Mansion, she promptly fainted.

As soon as Mrs. Stevens regained consciousness, she grounded Starflyer indefinitely from all that she termed "nonsense"—the attic lab, the Starwagon, and most of all, Botty. Starflyer's father assured her that Starflyer would remain grounded until he earned perfect marks on all his quizzes and proved he was no longer interested in dangerous ideas. Orson Jr. even changed the locks on the attic door and nailed a few more crisscrossed boards across the doorframe so there would be no possible way for Starflyer to enter.

Seven gloomy days later, Starflyer waited until his father had left for the Ministry before he climbed out his bedroom window and shimmied up the drainage pipe to the roof.

From there he climbed down the skylight ladder and dropped into the laboratory. Thankfully, his inventions were still as he had left them.

Starflyer was just about to insert the token into the Power Slot when a familiar voice cried out from behind him.

"Master Starflyer!" Botty's voice screeched over the funnel-speakers of the lab. "Master Starflyer! Do you copy?"

Starflyer pulled the Wire from the wall. Its cord stretched across the lab as he climbed the skylight ladder up to the roof. He looked down into the yard below and saw Botty sitting in the driver's seat of the Starwagon, parked in the shade of a nearby pecan tree. She was disguised as a Hobbler, wearing old clothes given to her by Crump. Her mop string hair was hidden by an enormous top hat, and a long, black overcoat concealed her arms and legs.

"Botty!" Starflyer cried. "Where have you been?"

"Staying with Mr. Critchfield," Botty replied. "He is a brilliant man, Master Starflyer! There is much we can learn from him."

"Yes, but I don't know if we can trust him yet, Botty," Starflyer replied. "Just please be careful over there."

"Oh, but I am rarely at the mansion, Master Starflyer. Mr. Critchfield has me running all over town. I am his eyes and ears."

"Have I missed anything in town?" Starflyer asked.

"Oh my, yes! The Pumpkin Dance has been cancelled. No Pumpkin Princess this month! No trick-or-treating! And, worst of all, more kids have gone missing! Every day, a dozen or so more are reported having vanished from their beds! People are beginning to believe it's the *real* Vothlor.

They keep speaking about a similar instance which took place during the Old War, when dozens of kids in town vanished."

Right then, Starflyer heard a door slam downstairs.

"Botty, quick!" he called. "Look through the kitchen windows. Has my father just come back home?"

Starflyer heard her squeal, and then she cried out, "Someone is coming up the stairs, Master Starflyer! But it isn't your father! Hide! Hide now!"

Heavy footsteps pounded up the spiral staircase and stopped just outside the blocked doorway of the attic lab. Starflyer scaled down the skylight ladder and slipped into his secret hideaway behind the bookshelf.

At least no one can get inside my lab unless they climb in through the window, Starflyer thought, now strangely grateful his father had boarded the door.

All of a sudden, he heard a heavy thump slam into the door of the attic. It pounded over and over again, until the door began to give way. Whoever stood outside the lab was not discouraged by Orson Jr.'s crisscrossed boards, and continued ramming the door with something heavy and sharp. Moments later, the blade of an axe chopped a giant hole through the door.

A man in a dusty top hat stepped through the splintered opening in the attic door and rested the weapon at his side. He stood at least seven feet tall, and Starflyer noticed the stranger's teeth were black as the pebbles in Midnight Creek. The man walked directly to the farthest wall, and counted twelve floorboards. He lifted the axe up over his head and brought it down against the floorboards, ripping the slots to shreds.

79

The fearsome intruder fell to his knees and searched inside the floor, but the secret compartment had already been emptied. He roared in frustration, then grabbed up a piece of paper and pencil, scribbled a note, and jammed it into the hollow. An instant later, he was gone.

When it was safe, Starflyer walked out of the closet and plucked out the note. It read:

> *The Time Crystal best be here when I return.*
> *If it is not, I will kill you and your family.*

The bottom of the letter was marked with a blood-soaked **!**.

Chapter 20:

Strange Nuisances

Orson Jr. stood with his hands on his hips, staring down in disapproval at the wrecked doorway of the attic lab.

"Tell me what happened, Son—from the beginning," Orson Jr. requested in a soft, puzzled voice.

Starflyer relayed his rehearsed story. "I was in my bedroom studying when I heard something hitting the attic door upstairs. So I hid beneath my bed and came up here once I was sure the intruder was gone. I found everything as it is now."

"And you're certain nothing is missing?" Orson Jr. questioned for the fourth time. "Have you any valuables a burglar might be after?"

"Nothing I can think of," Starflyer fibbed. "Except my inventions."

Orson Jr. placed his hand on Starflyer's back and

guided him down the spiral staircase to the kitchen. He hung a cauldron of water over the hearth-coals to warm it for tea.

As the tea brewed, Orson Jr. took a seat at the kitchen table across from Starflyer. "Son, it's not the first time we've had a break-in. After my father died—*your* grandfather— several burglars came to steal his inventions. At least that's what I've been told. I was just a baby when he converted to the Vothlor at the end of the Old War, and lost his life."

It was the first time Starflyer had ever heard his father speak of his father, Orson Sr.

"My grandfather was part of the Vothlor? And—and he was an inventor?" Starflyer asked.

"So I've been told. Ran experiments on crystals, trying to find a way to travel through time," Orson Jr. replied. "I've found all sorts of strange things in this house ever since I was a boy. In the walls, up the chimney, even stuffed inside tree hollows, if you can believe it. Over the years I came to understand that these . . . unnatural tendencies were what lured him to the Vothlor."

Starflyer sat quiet.

"When I became a father, I vowed that this would never happen to my son. And it will not," Orson Jr. concluded.

"Dad, what if the burglar comes back for—" Starflyer paused, imagining the burlap sack stolen at the beginning of the month—the one holding the crystal decoy. "I mean, the burglar might come back if he thinks something valuable is *supposed* to be here."

"Don't worry yourself, Son. Our names are safe and sound in the Book Of Members. You are a Member of the Light, therefore you are immune to the Vothlor. It also doesn't hurt that your own father is the Director of the Ministry. Our faithfulness to the Ministry will protect us during this time of darkness." Orson Jr. lifted the lid of the cauldron and ladled boiling tea into a wooden cup.

He slid the cup across the table to his son, and continued in a soft voice, "I don't blame you for being concerned. These are strange times. Stranger than any I've ever seen. The missing children have us all puzzled. Not to mention that evil rock and the gruesome murders. And I heard—" Orson Jr. paused, as if afraid to speak his next words. "I heard a terrible whisper behind the Sealed Door again today."

Starflyer moved to the edge of his seat, and thought of what Twister had said at the Light Dock about receiving a message from the Old Director of the Ministry.

"Dad, what happened to the Director of the Ministry during the Old War? You've always said he disappeared, but where do you think he went?"

Orson Jr. took a deep breath, and sighed.

"The Old Director was one of the biggest traitors in all of Hobble. During the Old War, he was seduced by the voice of Malivar, and joined the Vothlor. He was even known to steal coins off dead bodies. As you know, the Ministry fell into disarray for many decades until I revived it."

"What was the Old Director's name? Starflyer asked.

Orson Sr. looked at Starflyer with a suspicious glance. "I've told you before, Son. We don't say the names of traitors in Hobble. I will speak no further of this."

Starflyer observed his father's lost gaze, and continued, "But I need to know. What was his—"

But Orson Jr. pointed to the cup of tea and interrupted, "Drink some vanilla bean tea, Son. Your nerves are understandably shaken. Better yet, why don't you go into town for a free taste of the Gubbles' brew? Those nice ladies have been asking for you at the Ministry. Just make certain to be home before dark."

Chapter 21:

Sipping From The Spoon

Due to parents' growing fear of allowing their children outside the house after sunset, the long, usual line of kids was reduced to a few eager tasters. Starflyer could hardly believe his own father had encouraged him to sample the brew, but Orson Jr. explained that he had recently befriended the Gubble sisters, who provided free cake and punch to the Ministry out of pure goodwill.

It was just before closing time at the bakery. Gertrude Gubble stood in the doorway, ushering the last few kids into the shop. She waved to Starflyer and blew him a kiss through the honeyed twilight.

"You-hoo! You're just in time, handsome boy!" she exclaimed, guiding him to the porch. "Come on in from the cold, won't you?"

Starflyer blushed shyly.

"I—I was afraid I wouldn't get here before closing

time," he stuttered.

Gertrude bent down and looked into Starflyer's eyes. She wore a red dress, and smelled of sweet vanilla sugar. "Well the sun hasn't set yet, and, besides, my sisters and I would never shut the door in the face of a handsome boy like yourself! Come along, I'll personally serve you up the free taste. It's your first, am I right?"

The last tasters of the day were leaning over a long counter and sipping from two wooden spoons held out by Vivy and Issa Gubble. The sisters refilled the spoons from a black cauldron, which bubbled over an open, blue flame.

"Right this way!" Gertrude instructed. "Take a place at the counter, darling boy."

Starflyer walked over and took a seat. He tried to peek inside the black cauldron, but it was elevated on a platform. The children at the counter clamored like eager puppies for the nearest spoonful, while the other two sisters playfully taunted them with their beguiling smiles. By the time Gertrude returned with a spoonful of the brew, Starflyer's mouth was watering madly.

"Be a good boy, now, and take a sip from the spoon!" she chimed.

Starflyer slurped up the most delicious, rich, unexplainable sweetness he had ever tasted.

He licked every remaining trace on his lips and whispered, "Thank you."

Something began to fizzle in his stomach, as he stepped down from the counter.

"I should be going now," he said, feeling strange, yet wonderful.

"Don't go yet!" Gertrude insisted as Starflyer moved

toward the doorway. "Have another taste or two!"

But Starflyer had already made his way around the corner and was walking in the direction of the Candletin Inn. A strange dizziness came upon him, and more than anything he wanted to return to the bakery, wanted more than just another taste of that brew. The alley fences seemed to pulsate, in and out. A high-pitched lullaby sang in his ears, and his eyelids became heavy like stones. With his knees wobbling, he stumbled against a nearby barrel.

"I told you I'd be back," a man's voice called out from behind Starflyer. "Now, where's the Time Crystal!"

Starflyer spun around and saw the axe-wielding giant in the dusty top hat looming over him. Then the rugged man jammed a sack over the boy's face.

When the hilt of his axe butted against Starflyer's head, the boy collapsed into the violent swirls of a strange, dreamless sleep.

Chapter 22:

Confession

"Wake up, boy," a sinister voice hissed.

Starflyer's aching head wobbled as he regained consciousness.

A blindfold covered his eyes, but he could tell he was chained to a chair. Heavy boots thundered against the stone floor. Someone was pacing around him.

"Where am I?" Starflyer asked groggily.

"You are far away from home," the man's voice replied.

Starflyer heard another chair scrape across the floor until it was positioned in front of him. The man gave a heavy sigh.

"I told you what I want," he said, calmly. "Give me the Time Crystal."

"I—I don't know what you're talking about—"

"Don't lie to me, boy!" the man shouted. "Where is it?"

Starflyer remained silent.

The man growled, "Let me be very clear. If you don't give me that stone, I will kill you and your family. Where did you hide it after you took it from the floor of your attic?"

The man took the blade of his axe and ran it gently across Starflyer's neck.

"I didn't move it! Someone else did!" Starflyer explained. The cold axe blade stung his neck. "A man came and took it from the floor. I never saw what was inside the sack. Never, I promise. I didn't even know the sack was there!"

The captor lifted the axe from Starflyer's neck.

"A man, you say? What did he look like?"

"He—he wore a dirty frock coat and walked with a cane. He had a burlap cloth over his head, so I couldn't see his face."

The man was silent—deathly silent—then whispered, "So, he's still alive. Where did he go after he left your house?"

Starflyer heard a door swing open above them, and a second pair of footsteps tapped their way down a creaking staircase. Starflyer recognized a familiar sound—jingling bells.

"What have you there?" the captor asked.

"Just a red cap," the Toymaster's voice returned. "I found it on my morning walk. But it's caused me some trouble. Sherriff Hopscotch came down here this morning with that nosey Cricklewood boy to accuse me of stealing the children. Said the cap belonged to Red Crisp—Harper's son."

"The last thing we need is the Sheriff to be suspicious,"

the man scolded Tobo.

"Not to worry, Silas. Everything came out clean," Tobo assured. "But I have to be going now. I'm running late for the meeting. Everything is coming together perfectly for Hallows Eve, just as the whispers have commanded. You should have seen how they all sprung to action when I told them the Old Director was set free, and that the candle has been delivered."

The Old Director? Starflyer questioned.

Starflyer heard Tobo walk back up the steps and leave the mysterious chamber.

"Now, where were we?" Silas continued, pulling his chair closer to Starflyer. "Ah yes, you were just about to tell me what happened to the Time Crystal."

"But I don't know anything else," Starflyer lied.

Silas pressed the axe blade against Starflyer's neck once again, drawing out a line of silky blood.

"The blood of a boy fetches a high price where I come from," the man threatened.

Starflyer remembered what Crump had said about the decoy crystal, and quickly spoke, "Alright! Alright! The next day I saw the burglar in the Hobble Museum. He gave the sack to the old fellow who lives there. Maybe he has what you're looking for."

"Cricklewood!" the man spat out the name. "He lied to me!"

The stranger threw the axe to the floor and unlocked the chains holding Starflyer to the chair.

Am I being freed? Starflyer hoped.

Suddenly, a gag was stuffed inside Starflyer's mouth, and the sack was pulled back over his entire body. The man heaved him over his shoulder and climbed the creaking staircase, emerging into the cool night where twelve deathful gongs of the Clock Tower rang out nearby.

I'm still near Town Square, Starflyer realized. *And it's midnight.*

The man tossed Starflyer onto a platform, then closed the hinges of a creaky tailgate. A quartet of horses whinnied, and the crack of a whip sliced through the air like a bolt of lightning.

It's a stagecoach, Starflyer panicked, noticing the purple hue of a lantern through the sack. *I'm being taken away in a stagecoach.*

Chapter 23:

Nightmares Of The Lostwood

Starflyer rolled around in the back of the stagecoach as the wagon sped through the Lostwood, bolting over fallen timber and cascading down hillsides. The wagon was filled with gold coins, and it jingled as it trundled through the dark forest.

Starflyer finally stood within the sack and tried to keep his balance. He squirmed inside the bag and worked his hands towards the laces of his shoes. He remembered an experimental addition to his sneakers he had designed a few years before, but did not know if the device would still work. He finally felt the laces on both shoes, and yanked up with all the force he could muster.

Nothing happened.

He yanked the shoelaces again, and felt a slight rumbling, but still nothing happened.

Once more, Starflyer jerked the shoelaces upwards, and

this time a slight hum started up, and his shoes began to buzz softly.

It still works! Starflyer cheered.

Tiny saws emerged from the soles of his shoes, and began cutting through the wood of the stagecoach. Starflyer turned in a circle, while the saws created an escape-hole beneath him. He feared Silas would turn and see him before he could escape, but the driver was too distracted by the crooked path of the forest road to notice. The wagon rattled through ditches and over rocks, muffling the sound of the saws' hum. Starflyer felt the blades cutting through the sack, and through the wood of the stagecoach, until . . .

Whump!

He had dropped through the bottom of the wagon and rolled across the ground, crashing headfirst into the base of a monstrous tree. The stagecoach clattered on, continuing deeper into the Lostwood, losing dozens of coins through the escape hole.

Starflyer quickly climbed out of the shredded sack and deactivated the shoe-saw. He rubbed his battered head and examined the haunted woods around him. The forest was perfectly quiet, as if waiting on him to make the first move. Starflyer reached down and found a sharp stick to protect himself from whatever lurked in the night.

Suddenly, heavy footsteps crunched somewhere within the surrounding mist. Starflyer whirled around with the stick outstretched like a sword.

But no one was there.

"Helllooo, boyyy," a shrill voice splintered Starflyer's thoughts. It was the same voice which had pierced him in the Light Factory and at the Sealed Door.

"Who—who's there?" Starflyer called back, jabbing his stick at the nothingness.

"I can giiive you poowwers beyooonnd imagination, powers yourr faaather forbids. In exchaaange for your soul, I shaaall spaarre yoooou the nightttmaaarres."

"Where—where are you?" he said. "Leave me alone."

A horrifying vision entered into Starflyer's thoughts. It was as if he were looking back upon himself as a cloaked vapor feasted on his own corpse. Starflyer cried out, but when the nightmarish being looked up at him, there was no face. Only a void. The image fled from his mind, and he felt cold sweat running down his back.

I have to get out of this forest, Starflyer realized. *Or I won't survive the night.*

He glanced around, but every direction looked the exact same. Starflyer turned the frames of his goggles and they lit up like lightsticks, casting a line of bright light everywhere he looked. He reached over and picked up one of the coins, and placed it inside his pocket. As he did so, a thousand whispers chanted the boy's name, shrieking to him of dark dreams and destinies.

Suddenly, Zappy Fizzler's wisdom came back to him. Starflyer looked north, where a single star burned whiter than the rest. The Hobble Star. He began to run in its direction, fast and then faster, until he finally saw the twelve twinkling lanterns of the Crescent Gates.

His chest heaved with fright and excitement as he ran for safety.

Tomorrow, Starflyer thought to himself. *Tomorrow, I'll tell everyone about the man named Silas. Tomorrow, I'll be the one who solves the mystery—and saves Hobble.*

Chapter 24:

Promises Can't Be Broken

An hour before sunrise, Starflyer awoke to his father sitting in a rocking chair beside his bed, staring at him from the shadows. He sat up and clapped his hands twice, which caused a lantern to ignite.

Starflyer's father looked at him with tired, red-rimmed eyes and said, "Son, you've had us in a fright for the past day and a half. We didn't know what had become of you! We thought you had vanished like all the other children."

"But Dad!" Starflyer began. "I found out who's been kidnapping the kids in Hobble!"

Orson Jr. leaned forward in his chair.

"Who is it, Son?" Orson Jr. asked eagerly. "Tell me everything you know. If the Director of the Ministry and his son solved the mystery of the vanishings, conversions would triple overnight!"

Starflyer cried out, "It's the man who drives the stagecoach with the purple lantern! He tried to kidnap me too!"

Starflyer reached for his labcoat on the bedpost and took a gold coin from one of the pockets. He flipped the coin to Orson Jr., who let it fall to his feet without touching it.

"I found that in the back of his stagecoach," Starflyer said.

"Do you remember a voice, face, name. . . anything?" Orson Jr. questioned.

"His name is Silas!"

Orson Jr. stopped cold and grabbed Starflyer's arm. "What name did you say?"

"Silas."

Orson Jr. shook his head in disbelief and uttered, "Impossible! Silas Critchfield would have died long ago!"

"Silas *Critchfield*!?" Starflyer repeated in shock. He cast his eyes to the ground, catching sight of the gold coin glimmering in the lanternlight. Only then did he notice the ancient symbol on the back of the coin was the same one carved into the Sealed Door.

"Yes, Silas was the Old Director of the Ministry. What did he do to you, son?" Orson Jr. asked in a fright. "You didn't make any dealings with him, did you?"

"No, no. He sealed me in a sack, wrapped me up in chains, and put me in the back of his stagecoach. We were miles into the Lostwood before I could escape!" Starflyer explained.

Orson Jr. arose from his rocker and paced the room, all the while mumbling to himself.

"Dad, we have to tell Mayor Humplestock! We have to tell Sheriff and the whole town! Maybe someone else has seen him, or knows where to find him! If we find the stagecoach, we'll find the kids!"

Orson Jr. stopped pacing and stood next to the window, gazing towards Town Square with his hands clasped behind his back.

"Dad?" Starflyer asked. "Shouldn't we go tell everyone? We could form a search party within the hour!"

When Orson Jr. finally turned around, he announced, "Son, we cannot tell anyone what happened to you. No Hobbler can ever know you were in the Lostwood. During these sensitive times, people need to have full trust in the Ministry. If anyone found out my son was in the Lostwood—with Silas Critchfield, of all people—it would ruin my witness for the Light. Understand? My spotless reputation is the driving force of the Ministry."

"But what about all the chil—" Starflyer began.

"Let's just put this matter to rest, Son. Give me your word that you will never mention to anyone what you have just told me."

Orson Jr. offered his hand for Starflyer to shake.

Starflyer hesitated.

"Give me your word!" Orson Jr. demanded. When Starflyer stalled, Orson Jr. grabbed his son's hand and shook it. "There. Now you've made a promise, and promises can't be broken."

Chapter 25:

The Man Named Silas

Starflyer sat atop a stack of tall books in the Moontower, feeling sympathy for Crump as the old man struggled to understand the tale he had just been told. Starflyer had explained everything he had experienced that month—from the Sealed Door to the stagecoach with the purple lantern. Crump closed his eyes and deeply sighed when he heard the name he never wished to hear again: *Silas.*

"Mr. Critchfield? I mean, Crump?" Starflyer asked. "Are you okay? I thought I should ask you about it before anyone else."

Crump walked over towards Starflyer and piled a dozen books so that he could have a seat next to the boy.

"Silas Critchfield was my father. Even before he turned to the Vothlor, he was the most rotten man I ever knew,"

Crump said. "Rotten from the inside out, if you can understand that."

"I think I understand," Starflyer replied softly, remembering the feeling of a cold axe blade on his throat. "But if he was so bad, how did he ever become Director of the Ministry?"

Crump smirked. "I don't think I have to tell you that the Ministry is not always what it appears to be. My father had a gift with persuasion, and Hobblers trusted him."

"What happened?" Starflyer asked.

Crump sighed, and touched his deformed face.

"It occurred at the end of the Old War. I was hailed as a hero by then—one of the Five Warriors. And my father, well, he had not been seen for some time. Most believed he was on a pilgrimage to the Well Of Light to try to find a way to defeat the Vothlor and save Hobble—a naïve suspicion, it proved to be. But one night, I received a letter from him, asking me to meet him at the Ministry—in the room behind the Sealed Door. I, of course, being his obedient son, went to meet him. And that's when it all happened."

"What?" Starflyer asked, feeling his stomach twisting into a knot at Crump's tale.

"His betrayal. He not only betrayed the town and all those devoted to the Ministry, he betrayed me—his own son. Malivar, the dark vapor who had destroyed most of Hobble by then, was there in the room behind the Sealed Door. Alive. Blazing. Wickedly silent. The Black Candle was lit, and my father—my greedy, black-hearted father—sat there with a smile, looking upon me as if it were my birthday. He slowly turned to the cloaked vapor, and bowed. Immediately, I felt myself transforming. My body ached all over, and I looked down to see my hands changing shape and color. Soon, my hair began falling out, and I felt my skull bulging, until, alas, I was the decrepit, twisted creature who stands before you now."

Starflyer was no longer shocked by Crump's appearance, but he felt great sympathy for the man. He noticed the burlap mask lying on a moth-eaten sofa, and tried to imagine how much suffering Crump had endured.

Crump continued, "You see, my father had made a deal with Malivar. The cloaked vapor had promised him immortal youth if he was willing to sacrifice the youth and beauty of his own son. It was the price Malivar demanded in order for my father to prove his loyalty to the Vothlor. He left me for dead—and still believes I'm dead to this day."

Starflyer remembered what he had told Silas while being interrogated, and he wondered if he should tell Crump that Silas knew Crump to be alive.

"My father then spread the rumors around town that I had taken my own life in the mansion, driven to such insanity by the nightmares of Malivar. So I know well what it's like to be the son of a Director, young Stevens. I know that terrible feeling you get in your stomach every time you enter the Ministry. I know well what it's like to be the son of a man so hungry for power and control, that he would cripple his own son to gain his desire."

Starflyer sat, horrified. Despite his own father's flaws, he knew Orson Jr. would never betray him in such a way.

"Your father made you this way, so that he could be forever young?" Starflyer asked.

Crump nodded.

"But what about your mother? Didn't she—"

Crump's eyebrows furrowed and his jaws clenched shut. His flaky hands balled into fists. "Just because I tell you these things, young Stevens, doesn't give you the privilege to know everything there is to know about me."

"I didn't mean—"

"You must realize that some events in my life can never be revisited. Do you understand? Some things are even more painful than my father's betrayal."

Starflyer nodded. He looked across the room to Botty, who was secretly listening in on the conversation as well. Starflyer stood up and walked over to the fireplace to warm his hands. The house was constantly chilled by the cold drafts of October winds.

"I'm sorry, Mr. Critchfield," Starflyer said. "It's just— I'm just trying to figure out what to do. If—if you don't mind, there is one more thing I'm curious about—what exactly is the Black Candle?"

Crump closed his eyes, dreaming back to the days so long ago.

"I know you are curious about these things, boy," Crump said. "And there is much that you will need to know when the time comes. For now, know this: stay away from my father. And stay away from that Sealed Door. I don't want to see you hurt—or worse."

Starflyer nodded.

"When was the last time you saw him—your father?"

Crump shot a dark glance at Starflyer.

"If he knew I was still alive, this is the first place he would come," Crump grumbled. But if he ever shows up here, I will kill him. It's the last thing I swore to him that night behind the Sealed Door."

Chapter 26:

The Missing Shipment

The next night, after double-checking his homework lessons, Starflyer returned to Darkwish Road to visit with Crump and Botty.

When he arrived, the Critchfield Mansion was patterned by a thousand tree-shadows, which swayed back and forth like wicked monsters. Jack o' lantern scarecrows guarded the front of the decrepit house, their eyes burning with secrets. No candles or lanterns glowed in any of the downstairs windows, but the creaking front door swung back and forth in the ebb of the October wind, daring Starflyer to venture inside.

He peered into the entryway and was met by the smell of smoldering fireplace coals.

"Botty? Crump?" Starflyer called into the darkness. "Is anyone here?"

His own echo resounded off the walls and bounced

throughout the mice-infested parlors.

Starflyer ran down the porch and over to the workshop shed at the side of the house. He slid the barn door open, startling a family of sleeping crows which flew out of the hole in the roof. The clouded moonlight poured a grey chill into the lifeless barn. But the Starwagon was nowhere to be found, and the Light Grinder lay where he had left it a week before. Starflyer walked to one of the dusty windows and looked out at the mansion.

A single candle burned in the windowsill of the Moontower.

The Candle has been delivered. Malivar will be here soon, Starflyer recited.

All of a sudden, a hidden door swung upward from the lawn just outside the workshop. Starflyer crouched behind the window and watched as a shadowed figure climbed out of the underground cellar and crept across the yard to the back door of the mansion. The intruder jostled the back door until it opened, then disappeared into the mansion.

For Starflyer, there was something distinctly familiar about the shape of the night caller.

He snuck out of the barn and crossed the lawn to the back porch of the mansion. The door had been forced open, and Starflyer stepped into the musty kitchen. He walked past an old dinner table and into a darkened sitting room, looking for the night caller's silhouette against the walls.

A mouse ran across the keys of an old piano just as Starflyer walked through a newly spun spider web. Somewhere in the mansion, a grandfather clock rang three times to signal the witching hour—the darkest hour of night.

Suddenly, the music box upstairs began to play. The notes poured down from the Moontower like a dreamy rainfall.

As Starflyer climbed the staircase which led to the Moontower, he heard two voices conversing somewhere above, growing louder as he made his way to the landing.

"You failed me!" Crump's voice thundered through the silence of the house. "We must have them all! Every last one, you understand? Hallows Eve is almost upon us."

Starflyer froze and pressed his back against the wall.

A second man nervously replied, "I—I did lose one tonight. But I will make up for it. Give me one more chance."

"I want *results*, not just another promise. Your word is worthless," Crump scoffed.

"I can finish the job," the second voice pleaded. "Trust me. The shipment will be ready by the end of the week. We're almost finished. Just a few more left to gather."

Shipment? Starflyer questioned.

"If you can't do what I've asked," Crump resolved. "I'll find someone who can. Now, before you go, take this letter and send it through your breezebox. Make sure it gets to Garth Cricklewood by sunrise."

"But you haven't sent a letter in fifty years," the night-caller replied in astonishment.

"Just do as I have asked!" Crump demanded coldly.

Footsteps thudded across the room, and Starflyer dove behind a sheet-covered couch as the door to the Moontower flung open. C.C. Pottleman, Administrator of the Light Mines, quickly ran down the staircase and disappeared into the maze below.

Starflyer was about to make a similar escape when he heard another voice in the room—his own.

He moved closer to the door, bewildered by what he heard, but certain it was himself speaking:

"I climbed under a wagon, and that's when Woody and Twister showed up and told Tog the candle was lit. A message from the Director, they said. It was the strangest thing, Botty. Tog had just told the conductor of the Light Train that he didn't know anything about a candle. But when Twister brought it up, he seemed to know exactly what they were talking about."

Botty's voice started, *"Perhaps he was lying to the conductor."*

"Yeah, but why would he lie about a candle?" Starflyer's voice continued. *"Why is everyone making such a big deal about a candle? When Twister and Woody mentioned it to Sistine, she was shaking with fear. And now this."*

A screeching sounded, and the voices sped up so fast they were unrecognizable. Starflyer remembered having the exact conversation with Botty on the roof of their house the night the incident at the loading docks had taken place.

She's been recording me ever since the day I picked her up off the porch, Starflyer realized, picturing the tiny black box fastened to her Light compartment. *Botty is Crump's eyes and ears!*

From within the room, Twister Rubix's voice spoke from the recorder at normal speed, *"I'm afraid the boy heard it all. He knows everything, except for where the ceremony is to take place."*

Nittle Nightbrook, the town librarian, replied, *"Not to*

worry, Twister. Hallows Eve is only a few nights away, and we shall soon see the fruits of our labor. No goggle-eyed nuisance can stand in the way of Malivar's return. The Toymaster raised similar fears about the Cricklewood lad. But once we receive the mark, we'll have no reason to fear mischievous boys."

A click sounded, and the voices stopped. The recorder had been turned off.

Botty's cheerful voice erupted from within the room. "That's the newest recording, Mr. Critchfield, straight from the Candletin Inn. I can gather more eavesdroppings if you like."

"Thank you, Botty," Crump said. "You've been very helpful to me. But I must get some rest now. This has been the darkest day Hobble has seen in many years. Nicodemus Cricklewood was a light, extinguished far too soon."

Chapter 27:

The Hermit's Fascination

Several days later, Starflyer returned to the barn workshop and found Botty waxing the Starwagon. Each of Botty's claws pierced through six soaked sponges as she shined the Starwagon. When enough wax had been applied, she detached her head from her body and used her mop string hair to spread the wax evenly.

"Why didn't you tell me you've been spying on me, Botty?" Starflyer called from the doorway.

Botty wheeled around, startled by the sound of her master's voice.

"Master Starflyer! What a grand surprise!"

Starflyer walked towards her. "A few nights ago, I overheard you and Crump in the Moontower listening to a recording of—"

"Yes, yes, of course," Botty interrupted while she

composed herself. "I can explain everything in just a moment. But first I have a surprise for you, Master Starflyer. Have a look at this."

"Botty, I can't believe you would—"

Botty opened her torso and pulled out a rolled-up document tied with twine.

Starflyer untied the string and unrolled the papyrus scroll.

"It's not finished, but it's a start," Botty continued.

"Botty!" Starflyer cried out, staring at the document and nearly forgetting his reason for the visit. Botty had created a brand new blueprint for the SX12. The diagram merely lacked the secret mathematical equations and chemical combinations known only to Starflyer.

"And that's not all," Botty shouted, rolling to a wall of stacked hay bales. She pushed the middle of the stack, and the hay bales opened up like a door, leading into a secret room. All the pieces needed to build the engine of the SX12 were there, newly purchased, and hidden safely behind the wall of hay. "Your starship is finally ready to be built. The Beyond awaits us!"

"Botty, how did you move all of this? How could you afford all the new parts?" Starflyer asked, astounded. He had already mentally prepared for another twelve Octobers of hard work and planning before the SX12 could be finished.

"She did it with a little help from a friend," Crump's voice called from the doorway of the barn. The old man smiled and hobbled across the dirt floor.

"Thank you, Mr. Critch—I mean Crump," Starflyer replied, blushing at the hermit's act of kindness. "I never expected—I never thought—"

"No need to thank me, boy," Crump said, placing his monstrous hand on Starflyer's shoulder. "I'm happy to help. Especially on a project such as this. The simple truth is that I believe in you, Starflyer. Besides, I have more tokens than I know what to do with."

Botty replied joyously, "Mr. Critchfield is quite taken by your genius, isn't that right?"

Crump nodded and continued, "So you want to build a starship, eh? Fascinating. Now I know why Botty calls you 'Starflyer'. Orson the Third is much too drab for you. I had already ordered C.C. Pottleman to deliver a wagonload of Unfiltered Light for your project. He's the only one in Hobble who has known I am alive all these years, and I have employed him generously enough that he's kept my secret. He runs my business errands for me, you see. Regretfully, he has failed me again. But, not to worry. We'll have you soaring through the stars in no time. No doubt, there is much to discover out there in the Beyond."

Crump took a step closer to Starflyer and placed his other hand on the boy's right shoulder. "Now, come inside for marshmallow cocoa and a roaring fire. We can warm our bones while you tell me more about your project and let me take a closer look at those diagrams."

"How delightful!" Botty cried at the promise of marshmallows—her favorite sweet.

"Or, maybe the three of us could go to Gubbles' Goodies for some cocoa and a free taste of the new brew instead. My treat," Starflyer offered. "You have to try it, Crump."

Crump's smile faded into a scowl as he shuffled to the

barn door.

Starflyer and Botty looked at one another in confusion at the hermit's sudden change of attitude. Botty shrugged.

"Are you okay, Crump?" Starflyer called. "If I said something wrong—"

Before existing, Crump turned and said, "I already told you, young Stevens. I can never again let anyone outside these walls see me—even with that mask over my face. Hobblers must believe I am dead, so that I may be left alone. Never ask me to leave again! Never!"

The hermit slammed the door shut and crossed the lawn to his towering mansion. The smoke swirling out of the mansion's chimney soon stopped.

Chapter 28:

Late For A Meeting

The next night was Hallows Eve.

As Starflyer drove through town, he could hardly believe the empty silence of the streets, lawns, and darkened porches.

He caught a glimpse of Notch Cricklewood pushing his bike through Town Square, holding some kind of rock in his hand. He wanted to offer his condolences for the tragic loss of Pappy Cricklewood—his father had conducted the funeral the day before—but Notch had already made his way toward the hill at the end of the dirt alley behind Trajik's Majik shop and Tobo's Toys.

It was my fault Pappy Cricklewood died, Starflyer thought. *If I hadn't told Silas about the sack from my floorboards being taken over to the museum, he never would have been killed. I should tell Notch I believe him about the stagecoach with the purple lantern.*

But Starflyer was on his way to the loading docks. He needed another sack of Unfiltered Light so he could begin fueling the starship's power cavity for preliminary testing. If he and Botty wanted to launch into the Beyond by the next Hallows Eve, they would have to work every night for the next month.

The Light Train had departed earlier that evening, and the wagons used to transport the harvested Light were parked in a neat line along the southern wall of town. Starflyer parked the Starwagon near the wall, hoping the docks would be abandoned.

But as soon as Starflyer stepped out of the vehicle, Tog Gockle stumbled out from behind a nearby wagon. His hat was pulled low over his eyes, shading half his face.

"Hello, Mr. Gockle," Starflyer began, his voice quivering. "I was curious if—I was hoping I could have another bag of Unfiltered Light. I know the Light Dock is closed, but—"

"The time has come, boy!" Tog said, revealing a scowl illumined by the Hallows Eve moonlight. "There's no use hiding now! The candle has been lit! Malivar will be here soon!"

The Dock Manager began hurriedly jamming a few items into his satchel.

"Malivar? But he was destroyed long ago," Starflyer said. He had never known Tog to act so strange.

"I must be going—mustn't be late for the meeting. The Director won't allow tardiness." Tog turned and ran from the dockyard, but tripped over a coiled rope and tumbled to the ground.

When Starflyer bent down to help him, he noticed several coins had fallen out of Tog's satchel—the same gold coins he had found in the stagecoach with the purple lantern.

"Don't touch those, boy," Tog said, scrambling to stuff the coins in his satchel.

The nervous man scurried away from the loading dock in the direction of Town Square, mumbling all the way, "The candle has been lit. There is no time. Malivar will be here soon."

After a moment of hesitation, Starflyer followed after him.

Chapter 29:

The Voice Of Darkness

Stepping lightly so that the crunch of fallen leaves would not give away his pursuit, Starflyer trailed Tog through the maze of narrow alleyways behind Town Square. The night was cold and a storm brewed in the distance. Tog walked only in the shadows, and did not slow down until he arrived at the back door of the most unexpected place in all of Hobble—the Ministry Of Light.

Starflyer ducked behind a watering trough and watched as Tog climbed onto the back porch of the Ministry and knocked a syncopated rhythm on the back door. The door creaked open on its own, and Tog stepped into the darkness.

Just before the door swung to a close, Starflyer ran from behind the horse trough and stuck his foot in the doorway. He peered through the crack and held his breath in anticipation. The inside of the Ministry was freezing cold, and he could see his breath funneling into the darkness. Only a few lights remained lit next to the opened Book Of Members in the empty lobby.

Starflyer slipped through the doorway and crouched in a shadowed corner.

All was perfectly still until a voice hissed, "Cooommme tooo meeee, Tog . . ."

Starflyer covered his ears at the beguiling sound. Each word echoed off the walls a thousand wretched times, serenading the Ministry like a choir of shrill-pitched ghosts. Starflyer's chest ached with a sharp pain, and he felt breathless in the presence of whatever power lurked in the darkness of the Ministry. He recognized the sinister voice from the Lostwood.

Tog walked through the lobby and into a connected hallway, seduced by the voice. Starflyer stepped across the Lobby and saw Tog pushing open the Sealed Door.

"Cooomme in. Thisss waaay," the hissing voice called again.

Bathed in a purple glow, Tog crossed the threshold beneath the circular symbol, then vanished into the forgotten chamber. Immediately, the Sealed Door closed and a glowing ⚡ appeared upon its grimy stone, where the Sacred Circle symbol had once been.

Starflyer had just decided to fetch Sherriff when he heard another knock on the back door, in the same secret rhythm Tog had used. The young inventor pressed himself against one of the lobby walls and waited.

"Open!" the hissing voice commanded from the end of

the hallway.

The back door in the lobby swung open and a man stepped through the doorway, accompanied by the sound of jingling bells. The faint light of the candles revealed the Toymaster.

"Cooome tooo meeee, Tobo . . ." the voice bewitched from the end of the hallway.

Tobo walked past Starflyer without even noticing the boy hidden in the shadows only a few feet away.

"Where are you, Master?" Tobo asked.

"Overrr herrre," the voice guided Tobo toward the sealed room. The door slowly opened. "The hour of my resurrection has arrived."

It's Malivar, Starflyer realized in horror. *He's behind the Sealed Door.*

Chapter 30:

The Black Candle

The Toymaster stepped into the chamber behind the Sealed Door.

Starflyer inched his way toward the door, placed his hand on its cold surface, where the glowing **V** was simmering, and pushed with all his might. The door swung open into an underground staircase, which disappeared into the shadows below. As he reached the bottom of the stairwell, Starflyer found himself in a magnificent room with vaulted ceilings and a dozen tunnel entrances. The entire chamber was aglow with purple light.

Tobo and Tog stood facing one another on opposite ends of a long table, where a single black, square candle burned with a black flame at its center.

"It is tiiime. Prepaarrre my cloooak," the voice repeated.

Starflyer looked around the room for the source of the

voice, but only saw Tobo and Tog. The two men stood bewitched by the black flame, like wolves entranced by a full moon.

"We are your dedicated servants," Tog declared. He fell to his knees in reverence, and Tobo did the same.

At this, the black flame rose higher and higher, twisting like an enchanted ribbon as it circled around the two servants, enveloping them in its dark smoke.

Suddenly, the black vapor stopped at the end of the table, and a grey cloak hovered across the room and wrapped around the haunting fog. The cloak took on the shape of a man, but when Starflyer tried to see who was beneath hood, there was not a face, but only a dark void.

"Where is Silas? And where are the others?" the cloaked vapor asked.

"They should be here any moment, Lord Malivar," Tobo promised, bowing his head in submission. "Those who have declared allegiance will not disappoint you."

A faceless darkness peered down at Tobo and Tog.

"Then prepare yourself to receive the mark," Malivar commanded. "Bow down before me, and you will become powerful beyond imagination. I will live in you, and my power will be your power . . . for the harvest to come."

Tog and Tobo bowed before the dark vapor, and the arm of the cloak lifted up, as if there were an arm and a hand beneath it. But there was only black vapor, like the drifting smoke of a campfire.

As the vapor touched Tobo and Tog's necks with its ethereal fingers, a fiery **V** singed into their flesh, sparkling to life, and remaining aglow in the dark room. They quivered under the pain of receiving the mark, but their faces held a countenance of satisfaction.

"I can feel it—like—like being reborn," Tobo said softly.

The cloak fluttered in the chilly drafts coming from the underground tunnels.

"The Black Candle must be melted down into countless votives, so that the dark flame cannot be extinguished again by the Hobblers. The flame must be divided, carried by my vessels, so that if one flame is blown out, the others remain alive. Now, are you prepared to carry out my will unto death?" Malivar asked.

"Yes, Master. Anything," Tobo replied.

A moment of silence chilled the room, then Malivar whispered, "Then you shall begin by killing the boy who followed you here."

Tog and Tobo twisted around to view the base of the staircase. They burned with rage as they caught sight of the Black Candle reflected on the green lenses of Starflyer's goggles.

Chapter 31:

The Coming Darkness

Malivar's vaporous hand reached across the room and up the stairs as Tobo and Tog raced after Starflyer.

Starflyer slammed the Sealed Door behind him, hurried down the darkened hallway, and into the lobby of the Ministry. But as he pushed open the back door, he slid to a sudden stop, paralyzed by who he saw standing just outside.

Twister and Woody stared up at him from the Ministry porch. Nittle Nightbrook, the town librarian, stood behind them. They each had the same **V** mark glowing from the flesh of their necks.

The wicked puppet, who had recently received his own soul apart from Twister, reached its hands towards Starflyer's face and shrieked. Twister shoved Starflyer back into the darkness of the lobby, where Tog and Tobo closed in on him like hungry phantoms.

"You must be lost!" the Toymaster threatened with a grimace. "The Ministry is closed for the night! No one is supposed to be here—not even the Director's son."

Starflyer tried to run, but Tobo wrapped his arms around Starflyer's neck so he could not escape.

"You've been sniffing around our business all October," Tog accused. "In places you don't belong."

"You've seen and heard far too much," Nittle added. "And I know just what to do with boys who know too much."

The Toymaster looked towards the Sealed Door, which was now wide open. The Black Candle's flame filled the doorway.

"We caught him, Master Malivar! What shall we do now?" Tobo called out to the dark vapor.

All waited in silence until Malivar's serpentine voice replied, "Bring me his heart!"

"I'll pluck it out myself, with great pleasure," Woody announced, reaching ten sharpened fingers towards Starflyer's chest. Starflyer felt the finger-knives pierce through his labcoat and prick his skin.

A wicked voice pierced Starflyer's thoughts: *Join me, and you will have endless powers. Invite me to live in you, and you will never have to die.*

He writhed under the pain of Woody's sharp fingers pricking his chest, and furiously shook his head to fight the voice entering into his thoughts.

Right then, the door at the back of the Ministry creaked open, and Starflyer heard the sound of staggering footsteps entering the Ministry.

Tobo's arm was still wrapped around Starflyer as he

called out, "Who's there? The Ministry is closed!"

Slicing through the darkness against the furthest wall of the lobby, someone lurked in the shadows.

The conspirators looked at each other in fear and excitement.

"Is it you, Silas?" Tobo called out to the shadowed figure. "We have a surprise for you. Remember that boy who escaped your wagon? He's here now, and I'll give you the pleasure of ripping out his heart."

The figure, veiled by shadow and silence, slowly stepped towards the evil clan. Strangely, Malivar's presence felt dimmer as the visitor approached.

Closer and closer came the dark figure.

Closer.

Closer.

A bright flash of light erupted in the darkness, and a flaming bag was tossed towards the feet of the captors. Everyone looked down in confusion.

"Silas?" Tobo called again. "What is this?"

Suddenly, a monstrous face appeared from the shadows. It was more wretched than any face the conspirators had ever seen—and it was certainly not the man in the top hat known as Silas Critchfield.

But Starflyer knew the face well.

"Run, boy! Run!" Crump cried out.

Starflyer wrenched himself free from Tobo's grip just as the paper bag full of firecrackers sparked and exploded throughout the Ministry in a rainfall of fiery colors. The conspirators dove to the ground to avoid the ricochet of the booster-candles and bottle rockets.

Starflyer scrambled out the doors of the Ministry and

into the haunted, stormy night.

"Get him!" Woody cried, pointing a sharpened finger at the fleeing boy.

Starflyer ran across the empty street behind the Ministry. He ducked into the alley next to Gubbles' Goodies and climbed into a tipped over barrel, hoping it would be sufficient cover.

Tobo and Tog stumbled into the middle of the street and peered in every direction, debating over which way Starflyer had escaped. The Ministry was still exploding with fireworks, ringing into the night and lighting the windows in wondrous color.

"Come out, come out, dear boy! I have a special secret to tell you!" Tobo cried out.

A tin can rattled down the street, and Tobo and Tog sprinted after the noise.

Starflyer checked over both shoulders, then pulled himself out of the barrel. Even though he could see the yellow light of the lampposts just around the corner, Town Square felt like it was a dozen miles away.

Malivar's voice invaded his thoughts again: *Join me, and you will have endless powers. Invite me to live in you, and you will never have to die. You cannot hide from me. I am always with you.*

Suddenly, leaves crunched behind him.

Starflyer whirled around, expecting to see the puppet and his master, but the alley and streets were empty.

"Hello boy," a familiar voice called through the rising wind.

"Who's there? Who are you?" Starflyer demanded. A whirlwind of dust spun between the walls of the Ministry and the bakery, making it all but impossible for Starflyer to see clearly.

Then, a silhouetted figure appeared through the swirling dust. It walked towards Starflyer as if it were born of the wind—as if it were Death itself, sent to steal away one more life before the twelve haunting chimes of the Clock Tower announced the end of Hallows Eve.

"Please no!" Starflyer cried out. "Let me go, please!"

The menacing figure raised a small club in the air above Starflyer, and brought it down upon his forehead.

The world spun in a dizzying dance as Hallows Eve faded away like a long, terrible nightmare.

Some time later, Starflyer awoke inside of another sack, chained and blindfolded. Close by, he heard the voices of Scooter and Stokely Scabbins.

END OF BOOK TWO

FIND OUT WHAT HAPPENS NEXT IN . . .

MoonSung
presents

THE WATCHTOWER SECRET
BOOK 3 of OCTOBERS

FROM THE IMAGINATIONS OF
J.H. REYNOLDS AND CRAIG CUNNINGHAM

ILLUSTRATIONS BY J.R. FLEMING

DARE TO UNLOCK THE MYSTERIES.
READ ALL FOUR BOOKS TO SOLVE THE VANISHING

BOOK 1:
THE
TIME CRYSTAL

BOOK 2:
THE
HERMIT'S MANSION

BOOK 3:
THE
WATCHTOWER SECRET

BOOK 4:
THE
PROTECTOR'S EMERALD

Become a citizen of Hobble!

Visit

www.theoctobers.com

to receive your citizenship papers and
enter the OCTOBERS contests!

MOONSUNG
presents

Author websites:

J.H. Reynolds: www.moonsungbooks.com

Craig Cunningham: www.craigcunningham.blog.com

Made in the USA
Charleston, SC
13 October 2011